LOSER TAKES NOTHING...

"Slocum!"

"Yeah."

"I've got a sportin' proposition," Burt said. "I got two sacks of gold in here and Ellie Mae. She's naked as a jay. Gold, and a beautiful woman. Why don't you come and get them?"

Slocum's face was grim. Burt had a vicious sense of humor.

"Sounds good, Burt, but what about your gun?"

"Here's the proposition. You come in here. We'll talk. I got something to say. Then we'll draw. Winner takes all—the girl and the gold...

OTHER BOOKS BY JAKE LOGAN

RIDE, SLOCUM, RIDE
HANGING JUSTICE
SLOCUM AND THE WIDOW
    KATE
ACROSS THE RIO GRANDE
THE COMANCHE'S WOMAN
SLOCUM'S GOLD
BLOODY TRAIL TO TEXAS
NORTH TO DAKOTA
SLOCUM'S WOMAN
WHITE HELL
RIDE FOR REVENGE
OUTLAW BLOOD
MONTANA SHOWDOWN
SEE TEXAS AND DIE
IRON MUSTANG
SHOTGUNS FROM HELL
SLOCUM'S BLOOD
SLOCUM'S FIRE
SLOCUM'S REVENGE
SLOCUM'S HELL
SLOCUM'S GRAVE
DEAD MAN'S HAND
FIGHTING VENGEANCE
SLOCUM'S SLAUGHTER
ROUGHRIDER
SLOCUM'S RAGE
HELLFIRE
SLOCUM'S CODE
SLOCUM'S FLAG
SLOCUM'S RAID
SLOCUM'S RUN
BLAZING GUNS
SLOCUM'S GAMBLE
SLOCUM'S DEBT
SLOCUM AND THE MAD MAJOR
THE NECKTIE PARTY
THE CANYON BUNCH
SWAMP FOXES
LAW COMES TO COLD RAIN
SLOCUM'S DRIVE
JACKSON HOLE TROUBLE
SILVER CITY SHOOTOUT
SLOCUM AND THE LAW

APACHE SUNRISE
SLOCUM'S JUSTICE
NEBRASKA BURNOUT
SLOCUM AND THE CATTLE
    QUEEN
SLOCUM'S WOMEN
SLOCUM'S COMMAND
SLOCUM GETS EVEN
SLOCUM AND THE LOST DUTCHMAN
    MINE
HIGH COUNTRY HOLDUP
GUNS OF SOUTH PASS
SLOCUM AND THE HATCHET
    MEN
BANDIT GOLD
SOUTH OF THE BORDER
DALLAS MADAM
TEXAS SHOWDOWN
SLOCUM IN DEADWOOD
SLOCUM'S WINNING HAND
SLOCUM AND THE GUN RUNNERS
SLOCUM'S PRIDE
SLOCUM'S CRIME
THE NEVADA SWINDLE
SLOCUM'S GOOD DEED
SLOCUM'S STAMPEDE
GUNPLAY AT HOBBS' HOLE
THE JOURNEY OF DEATH
SLOCUM AND THE AVENGING GUN
SLOCUM RIDES ALONE
THE SUNSHINE BASIN WAR
VIGILANTE JUSTICE
JAILBREAK MOON
SIX-GUN BRIDE
MESCALERO DAWN
DENVER GOLD
SLOCUM AND THE BOZEMAN TRAIL
SLOCUM AND THE HORSE THIEVES
SLOCUM AND THE NOOSE OF HELL
CHEYENNE BLOODBATH
SLOCUM AND THE SILVER RANCH FIGHT
THE BLACKMAIL EXPRESS
SLOCUM AND THE LONG WAGON TRAIN

JAKE LOGAN

SLOCUM AND THE DEADLY FEUD

BERKLEY BOOKS, NEW YORK

SLOCUM AND THE DEADLY FEUD

A Berkley Book/published by arrangement with
the author

PRINTING HISTORY
Berkley edition/October 1986

ISBN: 0-425-09212-7

A BERKLEY BOOK® TM 757,375
Berkley Books are published by The Berkley Publishing Group,
200 Madison Avenue, New York, N.Y. 10016.
The name "BERKLEY" and the stylized "B" with design are trademarks
belonging to Berkley Publishing Corporation.

PRINTED IN THE UNITED STATES OF AMERICA

1

Slocum had just pulled up his roan in front of MacReedy's Saloon in Ledville when the doors swung open and a taut, blue-eyed young cowboy came out and started toward his horse. The doors swung open again and a bulky, hard-jawed, mean-eyed man in a tight red shirt stomped out, his face twisted in an ugly sneer.

"Hey, Tim Brady!" His voice was harsh. "Gonna be a yellow-belly, like the rest of yore no-account clan, and run? Or you gonna stand and fight?" His hand was near his holster.

Tim Brady turned, his face tight, his eyes gleaming. "I ain't afeared of you, Rafe Dancer, and I look forward to the time to draw against you. But the time ain't now.

1

I'm under strict orders from my dad not to mix it, to get back to the ranch. We got cattle trouble."

A group of men had followed Rafe Dancer out of the saloon, expecting trouble. Rafe grinned at them, then spoke harshly to the young cowboy.

"Jest like a Brady. Blame it on your dad, 'cause you got no goddamn nerve."

Slocum's jaw hardened. He hated the way this Rafe Dancer kept pushing the kid.

There was no fear in the deep blue eyes of Tim Brady. The rosy-cheeked young lad seemed to be struggling between obeying his father and stacking himself up against this mean-eyed dog who kept baiting him.

Slocum watched with tight lips, sensing something unpleasant had crept onto this hot street in Ledville. The men on the saloon porch sensed it also. They watched silently, their eyes shining. Tim Brady made a decision and turned to his horse, lifted the reins.

This infuriated Rafe. His eyes slitted. "Turn, you yellow-belly, and pull your gun, or I'll shoot you down like a dog."

Brady froze. He turned slowly and stared at Rafe. For one moment, everyone on the street held his breath. Then Brady's hand flashed to his gun, but Rafe was waiting, his face twisted fiendishly, as if he knew the outcome. The bullet spat from his Colt and Tim Brady rocketed back as his own gun fired. He dropped with a bullet in his heart.

Rafe Dancer walked to the still figure, his gray eyes cold and unpitying. Then he turned to the men and said in a mocking voice, "Another damned Brady hits the dust."

He glanced around, grinning, but when his eyes met

Slocum's, they slitted as if he didn't like what he saw. After a moment's hesitation, he just shrugged, pushed at the batwing door, and walked into the saloon, followed by the men.

Two cowboys went to the dead man. "Poor Tim. Never had a chance against Rafe. Let's get him on the wagon," one of them said.

The other cowboy shook his head. "This is gonna break old man Brady's heart. Not many of them left. Jest Ellie Mae."

Slocum lit a havana and hitched his britches. He moved toward the saloon doors with a sigh. He had been riding a dry trail under a fierce sun, and he had a thirst. This wasn't much of a town for law, and he didn't care for what he had just seen—a man bullied to his death—but it wasn't the worst thing he'd seen in his time.

The saloon was cool, with a long wooden bar and four card tables. Three busty women in tight red dresses were relaxing at a table. They looked at him with interest. Slocum was feeling interested after a hard ride on the trail, and one of the girls, a redhead, looked pretty in her low-cut dress.

MacReedy, the barkeep, a red-faced, heavy-muscled man, came over and nodded politely. "Whiskey," Slocum said.

MacReedy filled a glass and put the bottle in front of Slocum. "Riding through, mister?"

"Most likely." He lifted his glass. "Slocum's the name. What was the shooting about?"

MacReedy toweled the bar. "Bradys and Dancers don't like each other. Feudin'. Too bad about Tim. A good boy, too young to go. Bad mistake to come in, especially when Rafe was here. Guess Tim just wanted some beer on a hot day. Turned out to be his last."

Slocum turned to look at a nearby table, where Rafe Dancer was playing poker with four big cowboys. He studied Rafe. The man had a broad-boned face with cold gray eyes, a thick, red-tipped nose, and full lips that naturally curled in a sneer.

Slocum considered. It was not his business. The world was a mess when a nice young cowboy, who had scarcely begun to live, was wiped out by a polecat like Rafe Brady. But a man couldn't stop all the evil in the world—there was too much. Best to try to keep your own head above water. Slocum lifted his glass and drank.

For the next few minutes he watched Rafe Dancer play. He seemed to be lucky, for he kept winning. Each time he won a pot he would gloat a bit, to make the loser feel more miserable. Slocum shook his head. The polecat sure had a winning personality.

Slocum turned to look at the ladies and realized that the redhead was smiling at him. She had green eyes and full lips, and was built petite, but with all her curves in the right places.

He started toward her when Rafe's harsh voice cut the air unpleasantly. "Say, cowboy—you in the blue shirt—how'd you like to sit in this game and lose some money?"

Slocum stared at him. Rafe Dancer's tone was sarcastic, and his smile was mocking. Everyone turned to look at Slocum. Clearly Rafe's feelings were not friendly. Dancer had seen dislike, maybe contempt, in the green eyes of the big stranger, and he didn't like it.

Slocum moved slowly toward the table. "Be glad to play, Rafe. But I don't aim to lose."

Rafe's smile was mocking. "What's the name, mister?"

"Slocum. John Slocum."

"Well, Mr. Slocum, you can be sure of one thing—you ain't gonna win." Rafe Dancer's teeth showed in a savage smile.

The men in the saloon, sensing that the entertainment for the day was not over, smiled at each other and moved closer to the poker table.

Slocum took a seat opposite Rafe, next to a beefy, red-faced cowboy.

"Slocum? Seems like I heard the name somewhere," said the beefy cowboy. He strained his memory, but nothing came right off.

Rafe scowled at him. "You didn't hear his name in a jailhouse, did you, O'Rourke?" He turned to Slocum with a mocking smile. "Not a good idea playing with a cardsharp."

Slocum stared. "You got a nice way with words, Rafe."

Rafe flushed. "Let's play poker, Slocum."

They played for a time in silence. O'Rourke caught a couple of good pots, then Slocum won a few, which put Rafe in a sour mood. "Don't like the way the cards are running," he said. "Lemme have them." He did a fast trick shuffle, which made Slocum alert.

"Old man Brady's gonna catch him a nice surprise, Rafe," said the player they called Willie, who had small dark eyes and a lantern jaw.

Rafe growled. "It's time we cleaned out all the Bradys. All but one." His eyes gleamed.

"Be thinkin' of Ellie Mae?" said Willie with a grin.

Rafe nodded. "Don't know how a good-looking filly like her got into a bunch like the Bradys."

Willie laughed. "Mebbe it was a cowboy passin' through, paying his respect to the lady Brady."

The men guffawed.

Slocum looked disgusted. Rafe glanced at him. "What d'ya think of our town, Slocum?"

"Great town, seems like a lot of the riffraff of the territory has settled here."

There was a moment of hard silence. Then O'Rourke laughed, which snapped the tension.

"Damned if it ain't true. We got a lot of lowlife in town." Suddenly O'Rourke slapped his knee. "Now I remember."

Rafe scowled. "Remember what?"

"Where I heard of John Slocum. Served with the Georgia Regulars, under Pickens. That right, Slocum?"

"I served under Pickens," Slocum said.

"Right. And I fought with the Carolina boys. Not far off. I've heard about you." He turned to the others. "One of our best sharpshooters. He picked off the blue-coat brass. A great eagle eye." He grinned. "Pleasure to play cards with you, Slocum."

The others looked at Slocum curiously, but Rafe scowled. He didn't like to learn this about a man whom he already disliked a lot. Still, Rafe thought, a man could be an eagle eye with a rifle but slow on the draw. And in Ledville, Rafe had never met a faster gun than himself.

"Are we gonna go over old times or play poker?" he growled.

They settled down to play and the luck of the cards

moved around the table, but it mostly bypassed Rafe Dancer. He was a bad loser, and cursed a lot, and once said darkly that since Slocum got in the game nothing good was happening to him.

Slocum grinned. "Maybe the competition's got tougher."

"Mebbe yes, mebbe no," Rafe said, his gray eyes cold.

"Funny thing," Slocum said to O'Rourke. "How it turns out that a man who's a bad winner is also a bad loser."

Rafe stared hard, then ground his teeth in rage. He would never take a remark like that from any man, but something in Slocum stopped him. Slocum's reputation as a sharpshooter was something to think about. He studied the man opposite him, the piercing green eyes in the lean bronzed face, the powerful neck over the hard, muscled body. Slocum handled himself as if he had rarely tasted fear.

Rafe Dancer had met a lot of gunmen and cut down plenty. He had a lot of confidence in his draw. But he always picked up something in them that gave him the confidence to pull his gun. He didn't like the feeling he got when he looked at Slocum. In fact, Rafe almost felt a quiver of fear at the idea of a draw. Somehow, from the moment he shot Brady he had felt sure he would tangle with this green-eyed stranger. Slocum happened to ride into Ledville, and didn't like the way the kid was bullied into the showdown. Figured it was straight killing.

Well, it was, Rafe thought, but the Bradys deserved killing. Trouble was, this Slocum didn't know it, and he didn't conceal his disgust at the way Tim Brady got shot down. That was why Rafe had picked Slocum up for the game, intending to humiliate him, maybe force him to draw.

But Rafe's mood of confidence was now gone. Rafe Dancer thought of his brothers, and wished they were here. Somehow, when the Dancers were together they seemed invincible. Still, he could call on support from Lantern Jaw Willie.

Rafe looked at his cards. Nothing, not even enough to bluff with. He looked at the winnings, mostly in front of the big stranger. Slocum's green eyes suddenly looked at him, and he smiled a cold, killing smile, as if he knew the kind of thoughts running through Rafe Dancer's mind.

Rafe poured a whiskey, downed it, and shook himself. Damned if he hadn't gone through a blue funk—he, Rafe Dancer, who never lost a shootout. He was the fastest gun in Ledville and had proved it over and over. Why then did he let himself get buffaloed by this slick stranger? Slocum had made a few miserable remarks. Rafe felt it made him look bad in the eyes of the men. He couldn't let Slocum get away with it.

First he would skin Slocum of his money, then he'd put him where he belonged. Rafe smiled wickedly, feeling a surge of the old confidence.

"Feels like luck's comin' my way, Slocum," he said. "Jest watch yore money."

Slocum nodded, his eyes cold. "Reckon you're gonna need luck, because your poker ain't that good."

Damn! Another remark. It seemed like Slocum was pushing for a showdown. Well, he'd get it, and pay plenty.

It took five minutes for the right pot to show. Rafe

pulled two aces, a jack, ten, and four. That was what he needed. He eased the betting higher, and Slocum stayed. He drew two cards, watched Slocum draw three.

Rafe bet fifty dollars.

Everyone dropped out but Slocum, whose eyes slitted. He examined his cards, then studied Rafe.

"I'll see that and up you fifty," Slocum said calmly.

Rafe exulted. He had this green-eyed polecat where he wanted him. "See you, and up fifty."

The crowd around the table watched tensely.

Again Slocum studied Rafe. Then he said, "See you and up fifty."

Rafe's jaw clenched. "Up fifty."

After Slocum put in his money he said, "Let's see this big hand."

Rafe laid down three aces, a queen, and a jack.

Slocum didn't lay down his cards, just shook his head, as if admitting defeat.

Rafe's face was mocking. "So, Slocum. You don't like our town, don't like our sense of humor. Won't be surprised if you don't like the way we play poker."

"No," Slocum said calmly. "Don't like it at all. Not the way *you* play poker."

Rafe's eyes glittered, aware the moment had come. He glanced quickly at Lantern Jaw Willie, then back to Slocum.

"What's that s'posed to mean, you lowdown polecat?"

"Means you play crooked poker, is what it means."

Rafe should have gone like lightning for his gun, but he didn't, just stared at Slocum, who was waiting. Suddenly sweat glistened on his forehead.

The saloon was dead silent. His friends were watching. Rafe knew he had to draw, and he would. He was the best, always had been, and he would put a bullet right between Slocum's eyes. His hand went down like a snake. It was coming up, and he felt the surge of power as it always did when his bullet was about to destroy what he hated. That was his last thought as Slocum's bullet exploded in his head.

Slocum turned to Willie, who had his gun out of his holster, the barrel pointing down.

"Drop it," Slocum said coldly.

Willie dropped it quickly, his lips quivering.

Slocum jerked his finger at the door. "Don't try any tricks," he warned.

Willie, delighted at his reprieve from certain death, turned and moved quickly out of the saloon.

The players were staring at Rafe, who lay sprawled on his back.

O'Rourke said, "Why'd you think Rafe was cheating, Slocum?"

Slocum turned up his cards: two aces and two jacks.

"I count five aces in the deck. Where'd the extra ace come from? Out of that fake cuff. I've seen a cuff like that before on a cardsharp in Kansas City." He pulled the money together. "This pot is rightfully mine."

O'Rourke shook his head. "Knew you were good, Slocum, but never figured you could outdraw Rafe Dancer. He was the fast gun in Ledville. He and his brother, Burt—they call him 'Streak Lightning Dancer'."

Slocum shrugged. "A man can be fast in Ledville, but slow in Tombstone. It all depends."

O'Rourke walked with him to the door. The men

talked together in low tones. "Staying in town or riding on, Slocum?" O'Rourke asked.

"Staying a couple of days. To ease up."

O'Rourke's brown eyes gleamed. "I reckon you got a lot to be careful about, then. Rafe Dancer has four bad brothers. Not in town right now, but they'll be hearing about Rafe. A mean bunch."

Slocum smiled. "I guess I'll get myself something to eat at Laurey's place. Feel mighty hungry."

O'Rourke shook his head. "You're a cool one, Slocum."

2

At Laurey's Home Cooked Dinners, Slocum ordered steak, corn, black-eyed peas, yams, apple pie, and coffee. Laurey, a lovely older woman with fine features, watched him devour his food with pleasure.

He looked at her. "Are you the one who did the cooking?"

She smiled broadly. "I'm guilty."

He put down the pie quickly and smacked his lips. "Any more like this?"

She brought him another piece.

The door opened and two men wearing black coats and black Stetsons came in. One man, who had gray hair and a square, lined face, nodded at Laurey.

"How are you today, Mr. Wagner?" she asked.

"I'll know after I talk to this gentleman." He smiled. "Mind if I sit down, Mr. Slocum?"

Slocum looked into his clear blue eyes and nodded. The other man, broad-shouldered and square-jawed, nodded pleasantly and stood behind Wagner.

"I'm Charlie Wagner, and this is Abner Jones. We heard about the fracas at the saloon."

"Got a full account of what happened, Mr. Slocum," said Jones. He looked pleased about it.

Wagner rubbed his chin. "Mr. Slocum, we were wondering about your plans. Are you riding through or are you planning to stick around Ledville?"

"Why were you wondering?"

"Tell you, Slocum. We were chatting with Sean O'Rourke, and he told us 'bout your background, your work in the army. How you handled Rafe Dancer." He smiled genially, as if what had happened to Rafe did not displease him at all.

"Fact is," said Jones, "we were hoping you'd stick around, and if you did, would you take a badge and be our lawman? Some of us businessmen would be glad to pay you a fine salary for long as you wanted to stay."

Wagner leaned forward. "Everyone's talking about your fast gun, and that's what we need to get our town straightened out."

"Fact is," said Jones, "we been trying to turn this town around. It's been a stopping-off place for drifters in the territory ever since the Dancers have gone bad. We need a fast gun to move these men out, so our women can walk the streets of Ledville without worry."

Wagner lit a cigarillo. "Whaddya say, Slocum?"

Slocum shook his head regretfully. "One thing I

don't aim at is a law job. I aim to be free to do as I please. Would be nice to help clean up your town. But, if you think about it, yours is not the only town crawling with lice. There's plenty. It's up to good men to get together and put these polecats out of circulation."

He lifted his coffee cup. "Now, I intend to stick around Ledville just because I'm in the mood. If the Dancers come looking for trouble, they'll find it. I'll be around. If I need help, maybe I'll pick up the Bradys, since they're feudin'."

Wagner shook his head. "All that's left of the Bradys is old Ed and his daughter, Ellie Mae. You jest saw the last young Brady, Tim, go down." Wagner puffed on his cigarillo. "You're a fast gun, Slocum, and I admire your nerve. But the Dancers are a mean bunch, and it's not the smartest thing in the world to be taking them on alone."

Slocum shrugged. "Rafe lost fair and square in a showdown. The Dancers got no beef."

Wagner grimaced. "They're a clan, and what hurts one hurts all. They'll be lookin' you up, Slocum, first they hear of what happened to Rafe."

"They'll do that, I reckon," Slocum said.

The two men stood up, and Wagner put out his hand. "Sorry that you won't be the law 'round here. Would clean the town up fast."

They nodded at Laurey and went out the door.

Slocum smoked calmly as he lingered over his coffee, which Laurey refilled.

"A fine dinner it was, Miss Laurey," he said when he paid her.

"Come back when you're hungry," she said.

"Hope to."

She looked at him and bit her lip. "The Dancers are a bad bunch. Keep a sharp eye out, Slocum."

He grinned at her and went into the shadowed street.

He took a room at the hotel. It had a wooden dresser, a pitcher and a bowl, and a bed with a blue coverlet. From the window he could see lamps in the houses on Main Street, and up above, the night sky glittering with millions of silver points.

He pulled a bottle of whiskey from his bag and poured a drink. Then he lay on the bed, his hands behind his head. Ledville was not much of a town, he thought, cluttered with drifters. A town, Slocum figured, deserved the kind of polecats it got. He'd seen a lot of towns, and only where stout-hearted men took up guns to wipe out the trash did they get a decent place for their women and kids to live.

He heard the light step on the stairs. Noiselessly he moved to the door, his gun out. There was a light tap on the door.

It couldn't be the Dancers. Not yet. According to O'Rourke, they were out on the trail, and didn't yet know what had happened to their brother Rafe.

Still, it paid to be careful. He stood silently at the door with his gun.

"Open up, Slocum, it's Addie." Her voice was soft.

It was the pretty, smiling redhead with the green eyes whom he had spotted at the saloon. How nice that she had tracked him down.

"Figured you might want some company." She came easily into the room. Her red dress showed deep cleavage. Her red hair fell in short curls around her head, and her green eyes looked boldly into his. She had a petite figure with fine curves.

"You figured right," he said.

She saw the whiskey, poured a drink for herself, refilled his glass, and sat on the bed next to him.

"Slocum, you did what nobody in this town could do," she said. "You outdrew Rafe Dancer. Let's drink to that."

He grinned. "Don't mind if I do."

She patted her lips daintily. He felt horny just looking at her, and gulped his whiskey.

"Fact is, Rafe was not very popular in this town. Most were glad to see him go."

"And why was that?" Slocum asked.

"A bully, that's why. The worst of the Dancers, except for Bad Burt, the eldest brother. He's one clever devil, and if I were you, I'd watch out for him."

"I'll keep it in mind," he said. "Why's he called Bad Burt?"

She shook her head. "He smiles and smiles, but he's the meanest of them all. Leader of the pack."

"Who are the others?"

"There's Seth, Joad, and Diggers. All big, bad, and poisonous. They weren't always like this, but lately they seemed to have gone bad." She sipped her whiskey. "They've done a lot of damage to the Bradys. Tim wiped out today. None of the Brady boys left, lot of kin gone, too."

"Seems like the Dancers have won this feud," he said.

"Not till the last Brady's gone." She stood up,

poured another drink, and again sat next to him. "It's a feud to the death."

"How'd this thing start?" he asked curiously.

"Don't know how it started. Some say with Clem Dancer, the father, who pulled his gun on Ed Brady. Don't know what the quarrel was about. Water rights, land rights, who knows. Funny thing, it's said they were great friends at first. Always visited with each other. It was when Clem Dancer got shot one night that the boys turned vicious and went after the Bradys."

"You'd think it'd stop now, after all this blood," Slocum said thoughtfully.

She shook her head. "The Dancers have taken a solemn vow to wipe every last Brady off the face of the earth." She sipped her drink. "There's beautiful Ellie Mae Brady. What in the world is gonna happen to her, one wonders? Up to now she's been protected by Tim and Ed Brady. Tim's gone. Town folk say the smart thing for them to do is to run down to Paso where the Bradys still have kinfolk. Still, I've seen Ellie Mae shoot, and she's no slouch."

Slocum nodded. He was interested in the feud between the Bradys and the Dancers, but he'd been looking at her, at her breasts and lips.

She picked it up. "Why are we doin' so much talkin' when I know it's not what you want?"

He grinned. "How'd you know that, Addie?"

"I can tell by what's happenin' right here." She put her hand on his crotch.

She leaned forward deliberately and unbuttoned his Levi's. "What a fine sight this is," she said.

They stood, and it took less than a minute for them to peel. Slocum looked at her with admiration. She had a nicely curved body, with a fine pair of breasts, pink-nippled and upstanding. Her skin looked silky, her waist slender, flowing into full hips. A fine woman, he thought.

As for Addie, looking at Slocum she was struck by the masculine vigor of his body, hefty chest, broad mus-cled shoulders, lean waist, powerful thighs and legs.

"Haven't seen a man more fit for lovin'," she mut-tered as he came close. His hand went over the smooth-ness of her breasts, touched the nipples gently. Then he stroked her back and buttocks while she took hold of him, caressing him over and over.

He pulled her to the bed, where she spread her thighs. His stalwart flesh went into her and when he reached his full length she moaned softly. As he moved his haunches, her arms tightened around his body, and she lifted her hips. They moved in rhythm, and for Slo-cum the pleasure kept mounting. Soon her body went into spasms, and she moaned. Again and again her body tightened as he thrust into her.

Now Slocum's excitement reached its pitch, and his thrusts became staccato and more powerful. When fi-nally he hit the climax, intense and searing, he clenched his teeth as the pleasure reverberated through him. Slowly their bodies stopped writhing and came to rest.

Slocum could feel her heart beating. He caressed her rounded silky buttocks. Finally he let go.

When she had dressed and was almost at the door, he said, "Wait." He put money in her hand.

She looked at it, then at him. "I been thinking it's unfair to pay me for the pleasure you've given me. But my need of money is greater than yours."

She lifted her dress, stuck the dollars into her stocking. Then she said, "Slocum, you make love like you fire a gun."

He grinned, dropped on the bed, and shut his eyes. Then the thought of the Dancers came to mind, but it didn't seem to bother him.

His eyes were shut and he was sliding into a deep sleep when he picked up the steps on the stairs.

Again came a soft knock on the door.

She's forgotten something, he thought.

She spoke softly. "Something else I wanted to tell you, Slocum."

The sound of her voice had a curious edge. With a quick movement he fluffed the bedcovers and pillow under the blanket, silently unlocked the door, and stepped to the side with his gun.

"I'm in bed. The door's open, Addie."

After a pause, a sharp kick flung the door open. Addie was pushed into the room, followed by Lantern Jaw Willie, who fired two shots at the bed.

Then Willie froze as he suddenly realized the bed was faked and that Slocum had to be somewhere else in the room. His eyes, wide with fear, slipped sideways, until he saw Slocum at the bureau, looking at him. Willie tried to smile and swung his gun at Slocum.

The bullet spat from the Colt and hit Willie right between the eyes. He hurtled back and sat down against the wall, his eyes empty.

Slocum glanced at Addie. She was white-faced.

"He forced me," she said hoarsely. "He was waiting outside. Forced me to go back. Said he'd stick his knife in me if I didn't lead him to your door. I hoped to warn you." She looked at the bed. "Reckon I did."

She smiled, then she looked at Willie. "He looks better dead."

3

The next morning Slocum rode out of Ledville, taking the main trail south toward the Sierras. His thought was to scout the surrounding trail, then return to Ledville.

As he rode along under the climbing sun, he couldn't help thinking about Lantern Jaw Willie who, in spite of being warned, had tried a sneak attack in the hotel room. Willie had either had a strong sense of loyalty to Rafe Dancer or else he feared retribution by the other Dancers for failing to back up Rafe. If he feared the Dancers, it meant they would be vicious in their revenge.

Slocum was sure the Dancers would come hard after him, even though the showdown with Rafe had been square. He suspected that, for men like the Dancers, the blood tie was the most precious. They would ignore the laws of man.

So he had to figure the Dancers, once they got wind of what had happened to Rafe, would try to make him pay blood for blood.

Unfortunately, the Bradys had been thinned down, according to Wagner, to just the father and daughter. Not much for Slocum to count on.

The smart thing to do, Slocum reflected, would be to keep riding, put distance between himself and Ledville. But he was not a man to run from a fight. His instinct was to make the best of whatever circumstances he found himself in.

He thought of Addie and smiled. Might be amusing to play a game or two with her before he left Ledville. No, he was not going to run just because the Dancers were a mean bunch. He didn't know how to run, anyway. He made careful moves, yes, but he didn't run.

As he rode, he looked at the land. Trees and shrubs, jutting crags, hills and valleys. In the distance the Sierras loomed majestically, their peaks jabbing at the blue, cloudless sky like thin needles.

He pleasured in the view and in the smooth stride of the roan. He looked at the great rippling muscles, and patted his flanks with affection. He pleasured, too, in the sense of freedom that came when he rode the trail under God's sky.

Toward noon the summer heat beat down like a hammer on him and the flanks of the roan glistened with sweat. Slocum rode to a stand of shady cottonwoods near the crest of a hill. He dismounted, poured water in his hat for the roan, then sprawled against a tree trunk for what he expected to be a couple of minutes of rest. But his eyes, tired from the glare of the sun, slipped shut, and time went a bit strange. Because he began to dream, not seeing anyone, but hearing skirmishing and then voices.

"Took a long time, Brady," a man's voice said, "but I finally got you nailed."

"What you gonna do, Seth? Shoot me in cold blood in front of Ellie Mae?"

"No, old man. That's too easy. I'm gonna hit you so it hurts worse than dyin'."

Slocum, in the depths of his sluggish brain, foggily thought the dream was mighty strange. Seth and Ellie Mae, Brady—he knew the names. Were they part of a dream? If so, why did his ears pick up the sound so clearly?

Then Brady spoke in a hoarse voice. "I knew you Dancers were a lowdown bunch, but never figgered you'd stoop this low. Ellie Mae is an innocent girl. She's had no part in the trouble between our families. Just shoot me. I'm ready to go. I've seen too much rotten in the world. But don't touch her, Seth. It'd be the worst sin in the book."

Slocum's mind floated up from the depths and his eyes snapped open. Some freak of wind was carrying these voices up from the bottom of the hill; what he'd been hearing was real.

By taking the main trail south he had stumbled into another encounter between the Bradys and the Dancers. Fate seemed to be pushing him into the feud, whether he wanted it or not.

Then he heard Seth's voice, exultant. "Oh, I'm gonna touch her, old man. Jest like I figgered, it's the best way to hit you. And while I do it, you keep thinking of all the hurt you laid on the Dancers."

No dream, Slocum thought, and he pulled his gun and started to crawl to the edge of the ledge.

"If you touch me," said a woman's voice, throaty and intense, "I'm gonna surely kill you."

"How you gonna do that, Ellie Mae? I got the gun, and you got nuthin'. Nuthin' but that beautiful body, which I aim to enjoy right in front of yore daddy."

At the edge of the hill, Slocum looked down. A craggy-faced rancher in a Stetson was tied to a tree. Standing nearby was a rangy, ruddy cowboy wearing buckskins, gun in hand. Close to him stood a young woman, her hands tied. Her hair was golden, her face pretty, but just now distorted by anger.

The big cowboy smirked as he moved close to her. "Ellie Mae, I don't want to knock you around, yore too cute for that. But I reckon if I have to, I will. I wanta hurt yore dad, and yore the way to do it. Nuthin' is gonna stop me."

"If you do this thing, Seth Dancer, you'll pay with blood. I swear it," Ellie Mae said desperately.

Seth shrugged. "After all the blood spilt, a little more don't mean a thing. There's a river of blood already between us Dancers and the Bradys."

Saying this, he jerked at her shirt, tearing buttons. Her full breasts came into view.

"Don't do this, Seth," said Brady. "It'd be a terrible thing."

By this time Slocum had come down the ledge behind Seth. By crawling through high grass, he came to within twenty feet of him. He could see his gray eyes, brick-red face, and thin, bitter mouth. So this was one of the Dancers—Seth, a mangy dog.

"That's right," Slocum said calmly. "Not a nice thing at all."

Seth found himself looking at the barrel of a Colt held by a big man with powerful shoulders, lean hips, piercing green eyes in a sun-bronzed face.

Seth cursed under his breath. "Don't know who you are, stranger, but if I were you, I'd stay the hell outa this. Yore hornin' into a private feud. You got no business buttin' in."

Slocum's jaw hardened. Seth could not yet know what had happened to Rafe, nor could any of the Dancers. Slocum was in no hurry to pass along the news.

"The business I'm buttin' in, mister," said Slocum, "is you trying to take a woman by force. There ain't any grievance to justify that lowdown trick."

"Who the hell are you, mister?"

"Slocum's the name. John Slocum."

"Well, Mr. Slocum, jest haul yore ass outa here, because there's gonna be a bunch of Dancers 'round here. And you won't look good with a lotta holes."

Slocum shook his head. "You talk mighty fierce for a man facing a gun. It's clear you got more guts than brains. Now just drop the gun."

Seth grimaced, shot a poisonous look at Brady, at Slocum, then dropped his gun. "You win this round, stranger, but yore a dead man."

"I'll worry about that later, Seth," Slocum said calmly.

He came forward, kicked the gun toward the bushes,

pulled his bowie, and cut the cords that tied Brady. Ellie Mae came forward, holding out her roped hands. She was smiling broadly. Slocum was surprised at her eyes, cobalt blue, and the rich coloring of her skin. Under her golden hair, her face was finely boned, and she had a surprisingly full bosom for a young woman. The pink nipples were visible because of her ripped shirt.

"You're a real gentleman, Mr. Slocum," she said, "and I thank you kindly for this." She glanced down at her open blouse, blushed, then tucked it into the belt of her jeans, covering herself.

"Yes, Slocum," said Brady, "we're mighty obliged to you. And now, if I may suggest it, we better make fast tracks." He bent to pick up the gun, pointed it at Seth.

"Don't do that," Slocum said sharply.

Brady looked at him. "He's a mangy critter, killed my kin, and would have raped Ellie Mae if you hadn't turned up. A bullet will stop his career of crime."

Slocum shook his head. "We don't shoot unarmed men, Brady,"

Brady stared. "You don't know the Dancers. A poisonous breed. You heard him, what he was gonna do to Ellie Mae. Jest to get at me. And after he ruined her, he'd a shot me. What's the good of lettin' a polecat like him live?"

Slocum looked at Seth, his eyes gleaming with hate, his mouth in a cruel smile. He seemed to know that Slocum wouldn't let Brady shoot, and it gave him malicious satisfaction.

"Can't do that, Brady," Slocum said. "Just ain't sportin'."

"Bad mistake, mister," Brady said. "Ellie Mae, get on yore hoss. We gotta make fast tracks."

A grunt from Seth made Slocum glance up. On the top of the rise to the west were three bulky riders on big black horses.

"Reckon yore too late, mister," said Seth, grinning like a devil.

"It's the Dancers!" Brady yelled, and he pushed Ellie Mae toward a nearby boulder for cover. But it was too late. The Dancers, staring down from the hill, had already sized up the situation: their brother Seth roped, a stranger holding a gun on him, and Brady and Ellie Mae nearby. The Dancers fired. One bullet whistled past Slocum's ear and one hit Brady's shoulder. He dropped to the ground and crawled behind a rock. Seth grabbed Ellie Mae; she squirmed and cursed at him. Brady fired at Seth. The bullet hit his chest, catapulting him back. He sat down, put his hand to his bloody chest, and stared at Brady, his mouth twisting in a curse. Then his eyes went lifeless and he lay back.

Slocum figured that the Dancers would be fierce for revenge. He shot fast and sharp, his bullets whistling past their ears. The Dancers scuttled for cover.

"Let's ride!" Slocum called. Brady grabbed his pinto and swung over it, urging it fiercely with his knees. Ellie Mae swung over her bay and, as the horse galloped past him, Slocum jumped up behind her, firing back at the Dancers to keep them from accurate shooting.

"Take the left trail!" Slocum yelled. Brady swung his pinto around the edge of a stone cliff, which gave cover. Slocum figured the Dancers would stop to see what could be done for Seth, then to bury him.

Perched tight behind Ellie Mae, Slocum couldn't help responding to the firm curves of her buttocks. He wondered if, in spite of the shooting, she was aware of it.

But he couldn't spend time on it; the Dancers were a hard bunch with a strong sense of kinship. The death of Seth would surely spur them into vengeful pursuit.

Slocum directed Ellie Mae to the site where he had left the roan. He slipped from behind her, then swung over his own horse. They rode hard until he found a nook of boulders that offered good cover.

Ellie Mae, concerned, looked at her father. "Are you all right, Dad?"

"Jest a scratch," Brady said, and grinned. "Got no end of satisfaction putting Seth Dancer out of his misery."

Slocum examined the wound; it was superficial, the bullet skirting the flesh of the shoulder. He poured whiskey on the wound and packed cloth over it. Then he looked hard-eyed at the land behind them, but saw no sign yet of the Dancers. They had to be hit by the death of Seth, and must be involved in the burial. Also, Slocum figured, they felt confident that at any time they could pick up Brady's trail.

He pulled out a havana, lit it, then looked at the sunlit peaks of the massive mountain to the west.

"Can't thank you enough, Slocum," said Brady, "coming in the way you did. Mighty fine thing, sticking your neck out."

Slocum nodded, his face somber. Somehow, Brady didn't yet know about the demise of his son, Tim.

"Where were you coming from, Brady?"

"From visitin' with friends overnight in Bragg. On our way back to the ranch when, worst luck, we ran afoul of Seth Dancer. Somehow he picked up our trail.

That lowdown polecat got what he deserved." He rubbed his chin. "Yep, you saved my hide, and stopped Seth from doing something real bad."

Slocum puffed his cigar. "Wasn't gonna let him do that to Ellie Mae."

"I'd'a killed him sooner than let him touch me. Torn his eyes out," Ellie Mae said, her mouth hard, her blue eyes glittering.

Slocum looked sharply at her. She had a glimmer of steel behind her softness.

"I put a bullet where it belonged," Brady said, "in his rotten heart. Reckon you don't know what kind of men the Dancers are, Slocum."

Slocum looked away. Brady couldn't easily get over the fact that he had planted Seth among the daisies.

"You got a feud going. Means killing on both sides," Slocum said.

Brady's gray eyes gleamed. "Ellie Mae, me, and my son Tim are the last of the Bradys. In the fightin', I lost two sons, three kin, all killed by the Dancers. There was never a sneakier coyote than Seth, unless it was Rafe Dancer. You heard what Seth planned for Ellie Mae. He died too easy, if you want the truth."

Slocum was aware that Ellie Mae was watching him with narrowed eyes, as if she sensed something bothering him.

"I figure," Slocum said, "you did what you felt was right, Brady. We've got a bunch of Dancers hot on our tail. And they look plenty ornery."

Ellie Mae smiled. "The moment you pulled your gun on Seth Dancer, Slocum, you put the Dancers on your tail."

Slocum shrugged. The time had come to tell them.

"They'd be on my tail anyway. I shot Rafe Dancer yesterday in Ledville."

There was a long silence while they stared at him in amazement.

"Say that again, mister." Brady's eyes were glittering.

"Yeah. Rafe didn't like me too much, tried to cheat at poker and get a bullet in me. Had to defend myself."

Ed Brady grinned from ear to ear. "Mr. Slocum, I never heard sweeter news. Feel like you're one of us. I am beholden to you. Rafe was one of the most poisonous of the Dancers."

Ellie Mae came over and kissed his cheek. "Thank you for that, Slocum."

Slocum's face stayed serious. Looking at him, Ellie Mae suddenly paled. "What is it, Slocum? I think you're holding out something on us."

Brady turned to her and scowled, then stared hard at Slocum. "Something wrong?"

Slocum spoke in a low voice. "I'm sorry to be the one to tell you, but Rafe forced your son Tim into a showdown." He stopped.

Brady's eyes widened with fear. His voice sounded strangled. "Please . . ."

"Tim's dead. Some men took his body out to your place yesterday."

A strangled cry came from Brady. Then his face turned stony and his gray eyes stared sightlessly into space.

Looking at him, Slocum felt that Brady had just died.

Agonized, Ellie Mae rushed to him and put her arms around him. "Dad!"

Slocum looked at the faraway peaks, still glittering in the sun, looking like daggers aimed at the sky.

The stars glittered over their heads, big silver stars in the great dark sky. Slocum had dug a pit and made a deep fire to smother giveaway light. He had shot a jackrabbit and fried the meat. He'd served it with beans and coffee to Brady and Ellie Mae.

Brady, his spirits down, had been for going back right away to his ranch to give Tim a proper burial. Slocum persuaded him to wait at least until morning, when he could scout the Dancers better.

"To hell with the Dancers," Brady growled. "I yearn to get them in my gunsight."

Slocum rubbed his chin. In his rage for revenge, Brady could push them into a bad situation. The Dancers were three tough gunmen. It didn't seem smart to confront them with a girl and an old man.

"Let's jest get to my ranch, Slocum," Brady said, his voice gloomy.

Slocum exchanged a glance with Ellie Mae.

"It'd be fine, Brady, if it was just you and me. But we got Ellie Mae with us. Mighty risky for her."

Ellie Mae frowned. "I can shoot good as any man."

Slocum had touched the right button. As Brady stared at Ellie Mae his mouth tightened. He nodded slowly. "Okay, we'll wait till morning."

After they ate, they sat around the fire while Slocum cleaned his Colt.

The fire crackled softly, and every so often a night sound pierced the silence—the cry of a hawk as it struck a victim, the hoot of an owl, the slither of a coyote as it skulked through the bushes in its hunt.

Slocum smoked, and after a while Brady lit a cigarillo and sipped coffee.

"S'pose I oughta take Ellie Mae to Cousin John's place down in Paso," Brady said. "She'd be safe there. But I don't like the idea of bringing trouble to John. He'd be willing to help, of course. He hates the Dancers for what they've done to our people."

Brady sipped his coffee and stared at Slocum "You don't know these Dancers. Once they were a good breed of boys. I knew their mother, Martha, before she married Clem Dancer. Shoulda married her myself, but that's another story. The father of the brood, Clem Dancer, went sour one night. Came after me with a gun, challenging me right in front of his missus. Hadda defend myself. That was the first killin'. The Dancer boys felt I won the shootout unfair. They didn't care anyway —I had killed their father. Since then it's been the Dancers against the Bradys. I lost two sons, three kin, and now Tim, my last boy. There were six Dancers, countin' Clem. They're down to three. Burt, the oldest boy, took over the Dancer bunch. He's smart as a rattlesnake and just as dangerous. The Dancers have gone mean and bad just lately. Killing and robbing is what I'm talking about. I'm the last of the Bradys, and they mean to get me to square accounts. I don't know if Burt is vicious enough to take revenge on Ellie Mae. No tellin'. But the others, Joad and Diggers, are hard men. All in the grain of the Dancers, mean and bad. A pity it is, too. When they were kids they used to visit with us. Gone bad."

Slocum looked at the moon, a thin sickle that seemed stuck on the dark blue sky. A stupid feud, he thought, that started with a killing and built a thirst for revenge that couldn't be satisfied until one family or the other would be cut down.

And Slocum, mainly by accident, had got caught in the middle of the feud. He'd killed Rafe Dancer and indirectly was responsible for Seth catching a bullet. Whether Slocum wanted it or not, the Dancers had moved him into the feud. It meant he'd acquired three hard, dangerous enemies, and there would be no escape until he or they were dead.

Brady flipped his cigarillo into the air. "Yeah, I figger that come mornin' we'll ride over to the ranch, bury Tim, then head down to Cousin John Brady in Paso. That'd be best."

Slocum looked at Ellie Mae. It was sad that she was caught in this mess. Seth had been ready to abuse her for revenge, so it was a good bet that the other Dancers would do likewise.

She was a beautiful young woman and probably aroused not only the Dancer lust for revenge, but plain lowdown lust. Made it all sticky.

Forty feet away from him, Ellie Mae lay on her bedroll, the curve of her body enticing in the moonlight.

Slocum finally shut his eyes and slept fitfully through the night, part of his mind alert to any sound of threat.

Next morning, at sunrise, they rode northeast, making a wide skirt to come north of Ledville.

Whenever they reached a high piece of land, Slocum would climb it, his piercing green eyes scanning the trail for sign of the Dancers.

After three hours of riding, he picked up a slight moving blur. That would be the Dancers, three of them, coming hard and fast, and feeling vicious.

When Slocum came down from the high ground, Brady threw him a sharp look.

"Reckon they're comin'," he said.

"Someone's coming. Could be them." Slocum stared ahead. "Could be Sioux. It's their country, too. We stay on course for the time being." He glanced at Ellie Mae; her chin was stuck out and her mouth tight. A gutsy missy. "We'll look for good camping ground. Need to rest the horses and eat."

He picked ground on the side of a rise of craggy land, where a small spring drifted down from the high ground and a few boulders gave them shelter. It wasn't the best cover, but all he could find nearby.

He made a fire, put the coffee pot on it, and they ate beef jerky. Brady was silent, looking at Ellie Mae as if he had something heavy on his mind. He seemed to want to talk, but only about the feud.

"We're the last of the Bradys," he said to Slocum in a gloomy voice, sipping his coffee. "It's hard to believe what hate can do. And *we* never started this feud. It was always *them*. Wanting blood revenge. That's how Clem Dancer was built—a man who lived on hate. We Bradys were always defending ourselves. We had to kill to live. They forced us. I'm a peace-loving man. Never wanted much for myself, just a piece of land where our family could strike root. Now all my sons are gone, and most of my kin. There's only Ellie Mae, my one hope for the future. These Dancers are the worst kind of polecats. I've tried, again and again, to set up peace terms, but they never wanted that. Just blood. It's either them or us."

He raised the coffee cup to his lips. The sound of a rifle cracked the silence. Brady grunted and pitched forward, his eyes jumping. Almost by instinct, Slocum's gun was out, and he fired at a piece of the gunman hidden by the big rock on the hill. Somehow the Dancers managed to get up there, a hard climb. Slocum's bullet jolted the gunman, who jumped back. Slocum pulled Ellie Mae down, then flung himself behind a half-buried rock, scanning the land for another target. He saw part of two heads peering out from behind crags, and his gun barked, his bullets chipping stone.

From then on, nobody put his head out. Instead the Dancers seemed to have moved behind the crags, as if content with what, for the moment, they had done. Brady, the prime enemy, had been hit.

Slocum looked at Brady lying prone, a gleam in his eye, somehow still alive. Ellie Mae was weeping, her arms around him, as if trying to stem his blood flow with her body. Brady crooked his finger, wanting her to lean down. He was dying, but had something to say. His eyes glittered and his lips trembled. Ellie Mae brought her ear to his mouth and he began to whisper.

Slocum shot a look at the crags. The Dancers had moved back, staying out of sight, managing somehow to get their wounded comrade far behind the rocks.

Slocum looked at Ellie Mae. Her face twisted with pain as she listened to her father. A strange expression crept into her face, as if, besides feeling the pain of his dying, she was learning something bad. Her gaze dropped to the ground, then she pulled back to stare sharply at her father.

Brady's eyes gleamed with apology, but he seemed content that he had got something off his chest. It had to be mighty important, Slocum thought, for it took sheer grit to stay alive with a wound like that in his chest.

Brady glanced at Slocum, managed a small smile, then shut his eyes for the last time.

The sound of hooves pounding in the distance convinced Slocum that the Dancers were on their way. They had shot the last male Brady, and perhaps felt this ended the feud.

Anyway, it sounded like they were in a hurry to be somewhere else. It surprised Slocum, because he believed the Dancers were an unforgiving breed of men, and must certainly count him an enemy after Seth's death. Surely they would once they learned about Rafe Dancer. For that matter, he reflected, the Dancers were far from through with Ellie Mae.

No, they had urgent business somewhere, and when that was done, they would pick up where they had left off.

Slocum felt sure of it.

4

Big-bellied buzzards flew over them even after they had
buried Brady. The sun beat down on the dry, scrabbled
ground. Slocum mopped his brow and stuck his shovel
back into the saddle pack. He pulled out his whiskey
bottle and poured a stiff drink into a tin cup for Ellie
Mae.

She took it, her face pale, her jaw set hard. It was an
expression that he had once seen on Brady's face. She
was just like her father.

After she finished her drink, she looked at the crags
from where a Dancer had fired the killing shot at her
father.

"Wonder if it was Burt who fired that bullet. He's their best shot. They wanted Dad dead, once and for all."

Slocum looked at the mound of earth that covered Brady.

"I wonder," she said, "why they ran?"

"Maybe they figure there's no more feud now that the men are gone."

Her jaw clenched. "Not them. I'm still here. They can't like that."

He glanced away. The sun glowed with fiery heat over the peaks of the Sierras. "The Dancers may be a miserable bunch of polecats, but they are not going to shoot a woman."

She shook her head. "You don't know the Dancers. Seth was plannin' on rape just yesterday, don't you remember?"

His mouth tightened. It seemed hard to believe Seth had rape in mind. But if he did, then the other Dancers must also. They were cut from the same cloth. When you fought against the enemy, you didn't kill his woman. You took her body, which came to the same thing. To violate his woman was the best revenge.

He shrugged. She might be right.

Her beautiful blue eyes stared hard at him. "We're goin' after them, Slocum."

He had to smile. She was a gusty missy. "Listen, if you go to Paso, to your kin, you'd be safe. Wouldn't the Dancers figure it'd be too much trouble? And the feud would be over."

Her face was hard as granite. "The Dancers have gotta pay. I've lost my father and my brothers. I don't feel it right to be alive while they're all dead. Their voices cry to me from the bloody ground to square accounts or they'll never rest."

He lit a havana and wondered if this could be the right time to wipe his hands of the Dancer–Brady feud. If he rode south, toward El Paso, the whole feud business could fall into the past.

But could he ride away? He did want to help her. Anyway, the Dancers, when they discovered he'd killed their brother Rafe, would come after him hot and heavy. It was impossible to detach from this feud. He was part of it. He now had three vicious enemies—Bad Burt, Joad, and Diggers Dancer.

Slocum puffed at his havana. In truth, he would prefer to track them alone. Ellie Mae's presence could slow him down, make him too careful. He would always be thinking about how to protect her.

"I'll go after them," he said, hard-faced. "You just stay at your ranch and wait. Give me three days to nail them. I'll bring you news in three days." He smiled. "Or else."

She scowled. "What d'you mean? It's *me* that wants revenge. It's me that wants to see Dancer blood spilled. I don't want to hear about it sitting on the ranch. I want to see Burt, Joad, and Diggers destroyed—just like they did it to Tim and Dad, Jeff and Sam. I want to see their bleeding carcasses, just as I have seen those of my own flesh and blood."

Her feelings hit him hard. She was gutsy, and maybe she would not come out of this feud untouched. The feud would go on for her until the last Brady or Dancer was wiped from the earth.

Her blue eyes glinted hard. "I'm a good gun. You've

got nothing to worry about." She looked down. "As for you, Slocum, you're on their list. In the mind of the Dancers, you're one of the Bradys, whether you like it or not. You shot at them, and you killed Rafe." She nodded her head, unsmiling. "Better think of yourself as a Brady from now on."

He grinned and took the cup from her hand. "Suppose I just be Slocum, and put my gun on the side of the Bradys."

She stared at him. Her glance slipped to the grave of her father, her eyes misted, and her body moved against his for comfort. She sobbed quietly, leaning on his chest. He took a deep breath and looked at the crags, then west. The Dancers were riding west. Best to get started.

They rode through lush, luxuriant land, spotted with trees and occasional boulders. The mountain bulked heavy to the west. It was easy to follow the prints of the Dancers, who were moving unhurriedly southwest toward Abilene. But the land was tricky, lending itself to ambush, so Slocum studied the boulders, trees, bushes, whatever could serve as an ambush site.

The sun had started its downward trek when Slocum spotted two horsemen jogging directly toward them. He glanced at Ellie Mae, who was riding smooth as velvet on her bay. Her eyes had narrowed at sight of the riders but, after she realized they were not the Dancers, she stayed cool.

Now Slocum could see them clearly: one, in a beat-up short hat, had a sharp nose, quick brown eyes that moved from Slocum to Ellie Mae. He wore a dirty red neckerchief and soiled chaps. The other was stubble-bearded, with gray eyes that stared hard at Ellie Mae.

The sharp-nosed man tried a friendly smile. "I'd go mighty careful from here on, partner. There's a couple of angry Sioux out there ahead of you. We ran into them."

Slocum stared into his shifting eyes. "Do any damage?"

"Did plenty. Put an arrow right in the heart of Charley Mason." He pulled out a half-smoked cigarillo and lit it deliberately. "They call me Beaks. This is Blake."

Slocum nodded. "The name's Slocum. What's this about the Sioux?"

Beaks looked at Blake and grinned. "On the warpath, they are. Reason is these riders who came outa Ledville. They had them a young good-looking squaw. Dunno how they got her. Shot her brave, I reckon. So these two Sioux were on the warpath, lookin' for her. They happened on Charley, out hunting rabbits, and shot him. Blake and me were up on a hill, lookin' for water. Mighty lucky." He looked at Ellie Mae and grinned. "Where you folks heading?"

"Goin' to Abilene," Slocum said. By this time he had made up his mind these men were drifters, just picking up whatever they could wherever they could.

Beaks's eyes went over Ellie Mae's figure, and he licked his lips. "That's shore a purty miss you got travelin' with you, Slocum. Wouldn't be smart to let the Sioux catch sight of her."

Slocum looked at him coldly. "Where you headed, Beaks?"

Beaks shrugged. "Tell yuh, Slocum, we ain't in a

rush to ride anywhere jest now. We *were* headin' for Ledville. Heard it's a fine town."

Fine town for lowdown trash, Slocum thought. "Just keep ridin' east," he said, "you'll find Ledville. You'll like it."

Beaks took his hat off and scratched his head. "You don't aim to ride plumb into those crazy Sioux? Not smart." He smiled warily. "However, if you do, we'll ride along, jest to back you up, in case you hit trouble. Four guns are better than two."

Slocum smiled. "Mighty generous of you, Beaks, to make that offer. But I wouldn't want you to go outa your way."

Blake, who seemed fascinated by Ellie Mae, spoke for the first time. "Don't matter which way we go, Slocum. But I sho' hate to think this purty girl might fall into the bloody hands of those dirty Injuns. No, we'll be givin' you helpful escort."

Though Slocum's jaw tightened, he couldn't help being amused. It was foolish to think these scurvy polecats had nothing in mind but to give him helpful escort. What they had in mind was Ellie Mae. They could scarcely keep their eyes off her. It might be better, he thought, for the time being, to let things be.

"Besides," said Beaks, "we crave revenge for what they did to Charley."

"All right, then," Slocum said. "We accept your kind offer. If we get past the Sioux, you might consider wanting to ride on to Ledville."

"Reckon we'll think about it, at the right time," Beaks said, grinning at Blake.

Slocum glanced at Ellie Mae. She was calm, unconcerned, studying the land ahead of them, as if by trying hard she might be able to see the Dancers.

The sun started down and, as they rode, the heat seemed to lessen. Once, during the ride, Beaks tried to ease his sorrel into position behind Slocum.

"Best if you led the way, Beaks," Slocum said, "seeing as you know the position of the Sioux." Slocum had no intention of picking up a bullet in the back.

Beaks glowered a bit, shot a glance at Blake, then moved to ride beside him. The land was hilly and stony, thick with brush and spotted with boulders. Beaks pointed to tangled brush and trees far in front of them.

"That's where Charley got it," he said.

Slocum stared at the top of the hill, tangled with brush and trees, a fine place for a Sioux ambush. He looked at the ground. It was clear enough, prints of the Dancers, one horse hitting the turf heavily, the one carrying the squaw. And unshod ponies, Sioux trailing, determined on revenge.

"Figure on going up there," Slocum said, "to get a long look at the land ahead, before we camp."

Beaks frowned. "Why worry 'bout that now?"

"You got your friend Charley buried there, right?"

"He's in the ground now. Don't matter any more. Nuthin' to worry about. We just aim to pay off the redskins. No point in wastin' time."

Staring into Beaks's shifty eyes, Slocum felt that anything this dog said had to be a mouthful of lies. He just smiled and studied the ground nearby. There was a nice patch of land next to a huge boulder. It looked like it could give good cover, if need be.

He turned to Beaks, pointing to the boulder. "No waste of time. Why don't you two start a fire over there? That's where we'll camp for the night. Meanwhile, Ellie Mae and me will mosey up there and see if we can spot anything to worry about."

Beaks's face was grim. "Seems to me, Slocum, yore worryin' 'bout a lotta things that don't need it. But if it makes you feel good, go ahead." He turned to Blake, whose broad face looked stony, as if he didn't like what was happening, and was thinking of some private action. As if to head him off, Beaks spoke hurriedly. "Hey, Blake, there's no harm in it. Slocum goes up there, looks for redskins, and we make camp. We got the night. Nuthin' to worry about, right, Blake?"

His gaze was fixed hard on Blake, who squirmed a bit and rubbed his stubbled chin. "The way I figure it we should stick together, just in case the redskins try to jump us. They do that, yuh know. Then we got more guns."

"There's no redskins 'round here," Beaks said tartly. "Can't you read them tracks? They ain't new."

Ellie Mae looked at Blake and at Beaks, and then, as if she didn't give a damn what they had to say, she started her horse up the hill. Slocum smiled.

"That's that," he said. "The lady wants a view from the top." He waited, but the two drifters made no move. Slocum's face hardened. "So why don't you cowboys get a fire going so we can be eatin' by the time we get back." He reached into his saddlebag, drew out beef jerky and three cans of beans, and tossed them at Beaks. "That'll more than take care of our eats. We'll join you shortly."

Beaks smiled genially, but Blake stayed sullen-faced as they jogged toward the big boulder.

Slocum watched with narrowed eyes. About fifty feet

away, Blake glanced back, and Slocum, still watching, smiled.

Finally he decided it was safe to ride up. Soon as he could, he would have to do something about these mangy dogs. It had been a mistake to travel with them, but he never had the right setup. For Slocum, when a showdown came, everything had to be right. That was how he managed to survive in a dangerous world.

He found Ellie Mae on the hilltop where the ground sloped into a thick tangled underbrush, and the ground was marked with prints.

He studied the ground. There were prints of unshod ponies, of horses, scuffling prints, the dragged prints of a body, and finally the mound. It took time for Slocum to piece the action together. If you knew how to read the ground, he thought, it told a story clear as a book. As Slocum read it, his face hardened.

Ellie Mae had watched him bend to study the prints, following him as he moved into the brush until he found the mound.

"Would their friend Charley be there?" she asked curiously.

"It's him buried on top of a Sioux," said Slocum, grim-faced.

She frowned. "What d'you mean, Slocum?"

He smiled. "I'm gonna tell you what happened. It's all written clear as daylight. These three drifters happened on a Sioux and his woman. They shot the Sioux and grabbed the maiden. What I think happened was they were going to take turns with the lady, but she had a knife on her, and planted it in Charley Mason, who had the misfortune to be the first. Then she slipped away. Beaks and Blake buried Charlie and the Sioux, to keep everything quiet, then started to hunt her. What I figure happened then is that they saw her run into the Dancers, and wrote her off. Then they saw a couple of Sioux were looking for the brave and his squaw, and made tracks east. Ran into us.

"The two Sioux, from what I can read, had started to trail Beaks and Blake, but changed their mind and started after the Dancers, to get the girl." Slocum smiled at her. "Some of it is here, in the footsteps, the prints of the horses, the scuffling, and the grave. Down below, I picked up one of the Dancers' horses who rode heavy. He was carrying the Indian maiden. And behind them, the unshod prints of two Sioux." He paused. That's what I figure happened. Maybe not."

Slocum stopped, his face set in a grim smile. "From the beginning, I knew Beaks was telling a lie."

She shook her head. "Lowdown hyenas, aren't they?"

"We'll have to be careful from now on. They don't know that we know yet, but they are going to watch us real close."

He climbed onto the roan.

She looked at him. "You thinkin' of going back to join those hyenas? Why don't we just ride on after the Dancers?"

"That'd be nice, but how d'ya know they won't be following, looking for the chance to hit us, at night—in the back—whatever. It'd be better to join them, where we can see them."

She shook her head. "Hate it that we waste time with them. Can't stand being in the presence of such rotten dogs."

He shrugged. "Best put on a good face, or they'll

know we know. It will give them the edge. Gotta remember, there are two of them."

"I can shoot, Slocum," she said coldly.

"I'm sure you can shoot the eye of a squirrel. But this is something else. It's a matter of a fast draw."

She considered it, then grumbled. "Bad luck running into them, especially when all I want is the Dancers."

He shrugged. "That's the way it goes. You aim at one target and hit another. So let's just play our cards close to the vest and see what happens."

By the time they rode into camp, the stars were popping out of a light blue sky, and a bright quarter-moon was starting its ascent.

A fire burned in a pit, which proved that Beaks knew something about hiding his whereabouts at night. And the pan of beans sent out a nice aroma.

Beaks looked warily at Slocum as he came to the fire, and seemed reassured by the casual smile on his face.

"Smells good," Slocum said, "and we got a fierce hunger." He scooped beans and beef onto the tin plate, poured coffee into a cup, and gave it to Ellie Mae, then did the same for himself.

Though Beaks was eating, his shiny brown eyes never left Slocum.

"So, Slocum, did yuh see anything?"

"Reckon the Dancers have moved too far out. The light got dim, anyway. Couldn't see much."

"Took a long time to find that out. I tole you it'd be a waste of time."

"Did you find Charley?" asked Blake, holding his fork with beans in mid-air.

"Saw his burial place," Slocum said easily, thinking

it would be stupid to pretend he didn't see it. Everything else he might say would then be disbelieved. "Pity he got picked off by the redskins. We should hunt them down like dogs." His voice was a growl and carried conviction. Beaks looked at Blake, as if to say he'd been right, that Slocum would never figure out what happened on that hill.

Beaks had by then finished his plate and lit a cigarillo. As he smoked, he sipped his coffee "If you don't mind my askin', Slocum, what's there in Abilene that you and the girl are ridin' to?"

"We're riding to Abilene," Slocum said, "because the Dancers are ridin' there."

Beaks scowled. "The Dancers. Those are the three men who picked up the squaw."

"That's them."

"And why are you ridin' after the Dancers?" asked Blake, his gray eyes glowing in the light of the fire.

"We aim to kill them," said Ellie Mae coldly.

There was a moment of stunned silence, then Blake laughed harshly. "You shore are mixed in the head, lady. You're talkin' 'bout the Dancers. Bad Burt, one of the smartest, fastest men I ever heard of in these parts. And then there's his brothers, Joad and Diggers." He scratched his stubble beard. "So how does a filly like you and this lone cowboy aim to cut down them three big guns?" He shook his head. "I heard once they knocked off the bank in Fort Worth, shot up the sheriff and his men at Waco. The Dancers are mean guns. And here come you two, ready to wipe 'em out. Sounds sort of funny, don't it, Miss?"

"It sounds funny," Ellie Mae said, unsmiling.

"Maybe you would care to help us," Slocum said, "seeing these Dancers are such a bunch of polecats."

There was a silence while they all did some thinking.

"Why are you goin' after the Dancers?" Beaks asked.

"The reason is good enough. They just killed my brother and my father."

Beaks looked away. "Sort of sorry to hear that, Miss. But doesn't it tell you these Dancers are a mighty dangerous bunch? Nobody to tangle up with. I'm feared we can't give you that kind o' help."

Blake studied Ellie Mae, her ripe breasts and hips, and liked what he saw. He lifted himself on his haunches. Slocum got up slowly to pour coffee in his cup.

But Blake was not looking at Slocum. He spoke to Ellie Mae. "Howsomever, purty Miss, we can give you another kind o' help. I'm talkin' of consolation. When a gal loses her kin, she needs a bit of comfortin' and caressin'. Some lovin' is what I mean. That's what we aim to give. How 'bout that?"

There was a long silence.

To the right of Beaks, Blake had moved off his haunches and was standing, his body in a crouch. His eyes seemed to be on Ellie Mae, but he was watching Slocum.

"Only thing," Blake went on, "yuh might be hesitatin' because you got Slocum here settin' around, standin' in the way of you gettin' this comfortin'. Well, we aim to take care of that." His gray eyes glittered like coals in the flickering light of the fire.

Slocum waited, never taking his eyes off Blake. Then he said slowly, "Are you gonna pull your gun, too, Beaks?"

"Naw," Beaks drawled. "I'll let Blake do it. Gotta tell you, though, Blake's the fastest gun I ever seen, never been beat. So lemme just say, it's been nice travelin' with you, Slocum. Goodbye."

At the word, Blake smiled, as if the act of pulling his gun and killing was the only thing that gave him pleasure. His eyes drilled into Slocum's, because seeing the light of life go out in a man's eyes was the most entertaining experience Blake could think of. And his hand with astonishing speed swept perfectly to the handle of his Colt and was coming up, smooth as silk. But it never got to the level of Slocum's heart, because, by that time, Slocum's bullet had blown his brains out.

There was a sigh from Ellie Mae and a groan from Beaks, who saw his friend topple back, his eyes, sinister in life, now empty gray.

Beaks sat still, petrified, waiting.

Slocum's gun had shifted to him. "Now, Beaks, tell me what happened up on that hill. The truth, or I'll put a bullet up your tail."

Beaks's mouth quivered. "Don't know how you did that, Slocum. Blake was never beat before, not even near beat."

"They're never beat until they're beat," Slocum said grimly. "I asked you a question."

Beaks rubbed his mouth nervously. "You ain't gonna shoot a man who hasn't drawn?"

Slocum put his gun back in its holster. "You can draw."

Beaks's eyes went shifty. "I'm not interested in suicide, Slocum."

"Talk."

"We were up there, saw the young squaw with the

redskin, makin' love. Charley killed the redskin. He
wanted the squaw. She knifed him when he was on her,
then tried to get away. We dug Charley under, with the
Sioux, didn't want any of his friends tailing us. Then
started after her, until we saw her run into the riders.
Didn't want to tangle with them, so we went toward
Ledville and ran into you. That's it."

Slocum moved close to Beaks, pulled his gun, and
threw it into the bushes.

"Get your shovel, bury him, then get on your horse
and ride east. Maybe to Ledville. It's a good town for
you. Full of polecats."

The sun, a fierce yellow blaze in a drained sky, poured
heat down on Slocum and Ellie Mae as they followed
the trail of the Dancers. The flanks of the horses
gleamed with sweat, and Slocum was careful not to
wear them down. He kept the pace easy, making a point
to stop for water whenever he could.

The Dancers, too, as Slocum could tell from their
tracks seemed aware of the need for water.

From his reading of the tracks, which seemed only
hours old, the destination of the Dancers had to be Abilene. With that in mind, Slocum managed to make good
headway by taking shortcuts wherever he could.

Although the sun hit the earth with merciless rays,
the land still looked summer green, with thick, luxuri-
ous brush, and spotted with occasional dry patches. Tri-
angular rock formations rose from the ground in isolated
majesty, the print of eternity on their glazed surfaces.

When they would stop to refresh the horses, eat, and
drink, Ellie Mae didn't seem inclined to talk. Slocum,
looking at her, could still see signs of grief at the loss of

her kin. The hard set of her chin told him clearly that, born of the Bradys, she would only find peace when she had paid the Dancers, blood for blood.

She didn't appear to have much appetite and watched him stuff himself with fried rabbit shot earlier in the day. The gusto with which he put away the food seemed to irritate her.

"Can't understand you havin' an appetite like that, Slocum."

"Gotta eat to stay strong." He put another forkful of the browned meat in his mouth. When she pushed away her plate he said, "You should eat more than that, Ellie Mae."

"I'm eatin' enough," she said, her eyes fixed on him. "How long do you figger it'll be before we get the Dancers in sight?"

"We'll be mighty close by sundown. We'll be seeing them by tomorrow. They don't know we're after them, so they're traveling easy. They've got the Indian girl with them, two on a horse, so that slows them down."

Her jaw firmed. "That's what I'm living for." She kicked at a piece of wood that had jumped out of the fire. "I'm thinking now of that Blake. He was one rotten dog. Sure did disgust me, him talkin' of givin' me comfort. I'd'a shot him or myself before I ever let that happen."

Slocum smiled. "Figured he was kind of loco. There are men like that, go crazy to get a certain kind of woman."

"What kind of woman, Slocum?" Her gaze was curious, her mouth in a small smile.

He looked at her admiringly, at the smooth silk of her

cheek, the swell of her breasts, the sensual curve of her hips in her tight Levi's. "A woman like you makes a man like Blake go a bit crazy, ready to do reckless things."

She almost smiled, and looked at him thoughtfully. "What about you, Slocum? Would you do reckless things for a certain woman?"

He felt a surge of desire in his loins. Then he turned to gaze at the majestic mountains set against the scorched sky. It was pointless of him to have such desires in the midst of her grief, at a time like this, when she could be thinking only of killing Dancers.

"You're a beautiful young girl, Ellie Mae. I can't think of a man who would not do reckless things for someone like you."

"Someone like you," she mocked, and laughed, changing the subject. "Must say, Slocum, I sure liked the way you get that gun of yours out. Blake was a rotten dog, but he was fast. I feared for you."

Slocum nodded. "The main thing was I didn't have to tackle him and Beaks at the same time. Mighta been sticky."

Her face hardened. "They're both of a kind, Blake and Beaks. We don't need mangy dogs like them crawlin' the earth."

"No, but there's a lot like them, and how are you gonna clean the earth of them all?"

Her blue eyes gleamed. "We just do our bit, that's all. And it's the Dancers I've got my mind on."

They started again and, after three hours of riding, Slocum climbed a rise to study the land. It was then he saw movement, one horse and two riders. They rode slowly, and seemed headed for a small rivulet snaking through a stand of trees. Clearly they were headed for water.

Double riders. Slocum figured the Indian girl and a Dancer. He wondered where the others were. In a hurry to get somewhere? Why? He wouldn't think about that now. He studied the surrounding land to see how he could get behind the Dancer and the squaw.

His expression, when he came back to Ellie Mae, excited her. "You've seen something," she said.

He nodded. "One horse, two riders."

She scowled, then her eyes glittered. "Good. It's one of them. Easier to hit them when they're separated."

"Yes, might be easier, if we can get behind them."

"What'd he look like?" she demanded.

"Heavy-set, broad face, black Stetson, yellow vest."

Her eyes narrowed. "That's Diggers. Mean and vicious, like the others. He shot Sam, my cousin." She thought a moment. "It would be him doing bad things to the Indian girl."

"Diggers. Well, let's get started. I want to get behind him."

By now the heat had lessened, and he pressed the horses to move at a quicker pace. They rode north and made a big circle, bringing them behind Diggers. Finally they got good position, thick brush, tree cover, and grass where the horses could graze. He told Ellie Mae to stand by while he scouted. She didn't like it, but she agreed, provided he came back before he did anything.

He nodded, and moved quickly and quietly, climbing rocks which brought him to the side, from where he could look down to see Diggers and the girl.

Diggers was bulky, his body typical of his breed, bullet head, heavy-chested, thick-necked. He was standing facing the petite Indian girl. She had dark hair roped around her brow. Her skin was smooth brown, her legs shapely and strong. Slocum could see her finely cut features, dark glowing eyes. She looked tense, in a hopeless fury about the bulky Dancer in front of her.

Diggers pointed to the water and said something. She shrugged and turned from him. He grabbed her, pulled off her clothing, carried her to the water, and dropped her in. She squirmed, splashed, and came out, dripping wet, sputtering curses. She stood still, aware that her situation was hopeless. Diggers laughed, unbuckled and pulled off his Levi's, looking with a lustful grin at the girl. She glared at him, not knowing what to do, looking this way and that, hoping to find escape.

From his position on the rocks, Slocum peered down; it was a short climb to the thick brush on the ground. Diggers, by dropping his gunbelt to the ground with his Levi's, had made a bad move. His bulky body walked toward the girl, and he grinned in anticipation.

As Slocum climbed down, he was startled to see the girl grab her clothes and start to run madly toward him. Either she had seen him and thought he would help, or she thought the rocks offered a getaway.

Diggers looked stunned, then started after her until he saw Slocum and froze. Then he dived for his gun. Slocum fired at it, and it jumped and skittered away. Aware that this stranger might put the next bullet into him, Diggers stood still, hands at his side, his face truculent.

The girl looked astonished at the stranger. This big man, a sharpshooter who had destroyed that gun, didn't seem to care much for Diggers. She didn't know his intentions yet, but he was a paleface. He had a gun, and might be dangerous, so she, too, froze in place.

As he came forward, Slocum could read the fear in her eyes. He looked at her body, the high breasts, prominent nipples, dark hair between her sturdy brown legs. A beautiful maiden, he thought. He motioned for her to put on her clothes, and walked toward Diggers, who was watching him with a baleful eye.

"Who in hell are you?"

"The name's Slocum. John Slocum."

Diggers scowled. "Are you kin to Ellie Mae?"

Slocum shook his head. "Nope."

Diggers, looking hard at Slocum's face, saw no immediate menace. "Mind if I put on my britches?"

Slocum watched him slip into his Levi's, looking longingly at his gun on the ground.

"Leave it," Slocum said.

Feeling more confident with his pants on, Diggers studied Slocum. "Can't figure your part in this, mister. Why'd you follow us? Yore no kin to the Bradys. We Dancers got no quarrel with you. Why'd you put yourself in this? You had a gun on Seth. *Why?* Tain't yore business. And it can only mean a lot of grief." He paused. "Most smart folks in these parts don't tangle with the Dancers."

Keeping his gun on Diggers, Slocum pulled out a cigarillo. "Trouble is, it's you Dancers who tangle with folks. Like Rafe." He lit the cigarillo, thinking that the Dancers could not know that Rafe was dead. Not yet. When he ran into the Dancers, they were coming north of Ledville; no way they could have heard the news of Rafe.

Diggers's brown eyes screwed tight. "What d'ya mean about Rafe?"

"He played the cardsharp against me in Ledville. Too bad."

A glaze passed over Diggers's eyes, a small tremor over his mouth. His voice sounded hoarse. "What d'ya mean, mister?"

Slocum shrugged. "Rafe has gone to that great poker game in the sky."

Diggers's jaw tightened and he was silent. The loss of his brother seemed to hit him hard, but anger, too, seethed in his eyes. "That blasted idiot. I tole him, time and again, he didn't *need* to cardsharp. We can get plenty of money without that. But he wouldn't listen. *Wouldn't listen.*" He stared at Slocum. "Was it you who shot Rafe?"

"Yeah, me. After he shot Tim Brady."

Diggers socked his left fist into his right hand. "At least he did one good thing before he went, old Rafe."

"He bullied the kid into a fight." Slocum's voice was cold.

"No matter. It was a Brady, wasn't it?" Diggers said.

For the first time he looked at the Indian girl, who had her clothes on by now. She had been watching the palefaces talk, fascinated by the tension between them, aware that this stranger had done something that hurt Diggers. It pinned her to the spot because she hated him. For the moment, anyway, she couldn't think of an escape.

Diggers hitched his belt up as he did some thinking.

❖ "Listen, Slocum, if Rafe cheated on you, you were in your rights to hit him. Far as I'm concerned, you can go your ways. We got a truce." He paused.

Slocum had to smile. He had a gun pointing at this mangy coyote, yet Diggers talked as if *he* had the power.

"You're forgetting, Diggers, it's me that has the gun."

Diggers shook his head. "Mister, we are the Dancers. There's Bad Burt, Joad, and our kin, Luke Dancer; he's just joined us. Nobody can stand up to us, not around here. And they're sure to be coming back to see what's what. If you shoot me, they'll hunt you to the ends of the earth." There was pride in his voice. "That's how we Dancers are. We cleaned out the Bradys, and they were a hard bunch. Ask anyone."

Slocum flipped his cigarillo into the air, watched it spin and fall.

"If that's true, your brothers won't forgive me for putting Rafe to rest."

Diggers bit his lip, and Slocum realized the truth of what he had just said. It didn't matter what truce Diggers made; the Dancers would still try to hunt him down, for Rafe and for Seth. He wouldn't worry about that now. Mostly he was trying to figure out what to do with Diggers. Bring him to Abilene for trial? What judge would convict a Dancer, especially in a feud, where members of both families were involved in shootings. And the Sioux girl . . . what of her?

"Look, Slocum." Diggers's voice was earnest. "I'll vouch for you. It's true you got me at the end of a gun. But you ain't the sort who kills in cold blood. You let me go, I'll tell Burt, and we'll wipe off what you done to Rafe. Whaddya say?"

The girl started to move toward Diggers's sorrel, which was grazing nearby.

"As for the girl," said Diggers, his eyes narrowing, "well, she's a peach, isn't she? Trimmest little body in Texas. We can share her if you want." He grinned. "And since it's you who has the gun, you can go first."

Slocum smiled. "'Fraid not, Diggers. I don't rape women." The girl had stopped, as if aware they were talking about her, watching her.

Slocum smiled and motioned for her to go for the sorrel. Her eyes glowed, and she ran swiftly toward the horse.

"What the hell are you doin'?" Diggers yelled, aware that to be left out here in the heat of the day without a horse could be a death sentence.

He started to run after the girl. Slocum watched him. In spite of his great bulk, Diggers ran with surprising speed and seemed on the point of grabbing her. While Slocum was thinking of his next move, he heard the crack of a rifle, and a piece of Diggers's skull flew off as he pitched face down to the earth.

Slocum flung himself to the ground, as did the Indian girl. The shot had come from behind him, and he had his gun pointing, then brought it down. It was Ellie Mae, high on the rocks, holding the rifle to her eye, ready to shoot again, in case she had missed Diggers.

She came down from the rocks, her dark blue eyes glittering, her mouth in a hard line.

"What the hell was all that, Slocum? You had a gun on Diggers and didn't shoot. Are you with the Bradys or with the Dancers?" She looked at Diggers lying prone, blood leaking from his skull. Her face was cold and fearless, and Slocum could sense the flow of great emotions in her. She scarcely glanced at the Indian girl, who had stopped in her tracks. The girl, too, stared at the dead Diggers, and the expression in her dark cameo-like face seemed to be relief, because her tormentor had disappeared from the face of the earth.

She looked at Slocum, then at Ellie Mae, uncertain now of her next move.

Slocum pointed to the horse. "Go," he said. "Go."

Her dark face was impassive, but her coal-black eyes glistened with feeling. She put a hand over her heart and, moving with the grace of a fawn, she ran to the horse, leaped on his back, and rode east.

Slocum brought the horses down to where Diggers lay, pulled a shovel from his saddle pack, and dug a shallow grave. Finally he rolled Diggers into it.

Ellie Mae watched him with hard eyes.

"Told me you were only going to scout. But you didn't come back. So I had to come looking."

Slocum tried not to smile; there was a lot of steel in that soft-looking girl. "Couldn't help it, Ellie Mae. Diggers was going to rape the girl."

She looked into the distance. "You haven't told me yet whose side you are on, Slocum. You had Diggers and you didn't do a thing."

"I don't kill in cold blood, Ellie Mae."

"If you don't kill the Dancers, they'll kill you." Her voice was venomous. "You don't get a second chance. If you hope to live, you'd do well to kill a Dancer on sight." She started to her horse. "That's how they did it to the Bradys. Never gave us a chance. I'm the last. And I intend to be around when the Dancers are gone."

Her chin was high and her eyes glittered as she thought of her dead father and all her dead kin.

She reached her bay and swung over the saddle. In a harsh voice she said, "Now, let's get Burt and Joad Dancer."

5

Bad Burt Dancer sat astride his powerful black horse on the top of Redstone Pass. Along with his brother Joad and his cousin Luke, he looked south. They had a long, commanding view of the trail twisting to Abilene. It was a well-used trail, stomped flat by cattle. More important for Burt Dancer, it was also used by the stagecoach to Abilene, which, he had learned, would be carrying bank money and running past here by sundown.

He glanced at the sky, already orange as the sun worked its way down to the rocky horizon. Not much time.

Burt studied the land nearby and found pleasure at

the sight of three big boulders perched on the side of the trail. It fit neatly into his plan. He pointed to it.

"That's the place. We'll wait there," he said. Burt was the only Dancer who didn't have the family look, which was big, bulky, and powerful. He had the gray eyes of the Dancers, but a soft, round face and a short putty nose that stuck out over an upturned, smiling mouth. Not a face to inspire fear, but he was the most dangerous, because he was the smartest and fastest. His mouth seemed to smile even when he was in a fury. He wore a black Stetson, a blue neckerchief, and a tan vest over his Levi's. His steely gray eyes now looked east, from where he had come with the two riders beside him.

Joad, his brother, also looked east, biting his lip. He was built muscularly, with the broad, hard face typical of the Dancers, and bushy eyebrows over his gray eyes. "Where the hell is Diggers?" he asked.

Burt smiled, but the smile had no mirth in it. "He had to have that girl."

"Why'd you let him get mixed up with that Indian bitch, Burt? It was the wrong time," Joad said.

"How do you stop a fool from being a fool?" Burt asked.

"He shoulda been through with that by now," Joad said.

"Mebbe he likes her a lot," leered Cousin Luke. He was also broad-faced and muscular, with a knife scar on his cheek. He wore a battered brown hat and a soiled green vest.

"If it's female, Diggers never wants to let go," said Joad.

"Diggers doesn't do anything right," Burt said, looking at the sky. "It'll be sundown soon. We may have to do it without him."

Joad fingered his chin. "Think something mighta happened? He did say he'd catch up."

Again Burt looked east for Diggers. Nothing. His gray eyes glittered with a hard light, yet he smiled. Maybe it was to make you think he was friendly. There was nothing fierce in his face, yet he was feared, called Bad Burt Dancer, considered one of the most dangerous gunmen in the territory. He was a left-handed gun and he drew with lightning speed.

But Burt didn't use his gun much; he depended mostly on his brothers to do the shooting.

He was the oldest Dancer brother, and when his father, Clem, had been shot by Ed Brady, the mantle of leadership of the clan had fallen rightly on his shoulders.

Burt was thinking about this now as he cursed softly under his breath, scanning the trail for Diggers. Diggers was always at the wrong place at the wrong time, and usually doing the wrong thing. At the time their father, Clem, had been shot by Ed Brady, Diggers, in a rage for revenge, had fired up the brothers, wanting to stampede the Brady ranch, guns blazing. Only by pulling his gun had Burt been able to stop them. He was the cool head, convincing them that a frontal onslaught against the Brady boys, all fast guns, would only come to mutual slaughter. He sold the brothers on doing it slow and sly, which would bring them revenge and cost less in Dancer blood.

Burt's policy, of picking the right time for the kill,

had worked. Sure, there had been killings on both sides, but in the end victory came to the Dancers.

Sitting on his horse now under a flaming sky, Burt thought grimly of the Bradys, only Tim and Ellie Mae were left. And Tim might be gone, if Rafe had done his job right in Ledville.

For the last time, Burt looked east for Diggers. He was an idiot about women, always running his fool head off. It would be a woman one day who would plant him in the daisies. It had been bad luck when the Indian maiden had run into them, especially since they were headed for this stagecoach job. Diggers had scooped her up and put her on his horse, slowing them down. "Join you later, Burt," he had cheerily called, "at the Pass. I'll catch up."

That had put a knot in Burt's plans. He had expected Diggers, Rafe, and Seth to meet them at the Pass, but none of them had showed. It was a bad omen. Burt's mouth tightened. Seth was dead. Rafe might just be drunk in Ledville. There was no way he could lose in a showdown with Tim Dancer. He was probably sleeping off a drunk.

"What are we gonna do, Burt?" Joad asked.

Burt had been staring north at the tiny moving dot. *The stagecoach!*

His jaw hardened. "We're gonna do the job. We don't need anyone but us. We're goin' down." He pointed to the boulders. "We put ourselves behind the boulders. We're three, though I was countin' on five. Means we can't take chances. We shoot the driver and the shotgun guard right off. There may be a guard inside with the passengers. Watch for him. If in doubt, shoot him. We don't take prisoners. Anyone recognize us, shoot. That clear?"

Joad and Luke nodded, their faces grim, and they checked their guns.

They rode down from the Pass to the flatlands and got behind the boulders. They still had plenty of time, so they smoked and talked.

Joad took off his hat and ran his hand through his brown hair. "Diggers never let us down before. Reckon something happened, Burt?"

Burt's eyes clouded. Then the smile stole over his lips. "He took the knife from that squaw. I tole him to look for one. So she couldn't hit him. Only thing I can think of is that Ellie Mae and that big cowboy with her might have caught up."

Joad scowled. "Who was that cowboy? What's he doin' with her? Wasn't he the one with a gun on Seth, back toward Ledville? Figure him Brady kin?"

Burt shrugged. "Dunno. Looked like a dangerous hombre. Somethin' 'bout him. Could be *he's* why Diggers ain't here."

Joad grimaced. "Might be Ellie Mae more'n than him, if you ask me. She's got the grievance, and she can shoot."

Burt nodded. "Yeah. We gotta watch Ellie Mae. She may be a girl, but she can sting like a rattlesnake. Don't get comfortable with her." He looked carefully from behind the boulder, then flipped his cigarillo. "Better take positions," he said quietly.

Peering from behind the boulder, Burt could see the coach rolling along, pulled by four powerful horses. A husky shotgun guard sat alongside the driver. The driver cracked his whip hard over the sweating horses. He was in a hurry to reach Abilene.

The boulders gave good ambush position to the Dancers.

Joad and Luke sighted their rifles, waiting for Burt's signal. When Burt's hand went down the two rifles blasted. Almost at the same instant, the driver and the shotgun guard jumped, hit by the force of the bullets. Both fell in slow motion from the jolting coach, dead before they hit the ground.

The coach horses, terrified by the blasting sound, thundered on in a frenzy. Burt cursed as the coach swept toward them with runaway speed. The Dancers prodded their mounts trying to keep up, until Luke, lashing his pinto, reached the back of the jolting stagecoach. He clambered to the driver's seat and grabbed the reins, pulling them hard until the snorting horses slowed down and finally halted.

Burt and Joad, guns drawn, came alongside the coach.

"Come out," ordered Burt.

A woman came first, wearing a low-cut, shiny blue dress with ruffles. She had a rouged, pretty face, red lips, and hefty breasts. After her came a husky, red-headed, thick-necked man; he wore a black jacket and pants, a shoelace tie on a blue shirt. He packed no gun.

Burt looked hard at the passengers, then motioned to Joad. The younger brother found the wooden chest inside the coach and pulled it out. It had a bulky steel lock. Joad shot it and it jumped open. Two tied leather pouches were inside, and Joad pulled them open. They were filled with gold pieces.

"A nice day's work," said Luke, grinning ear to ear.

Burt smiled, then stared hard-eyed at the red-headed man. He was powerfully built and bulged in his city clothes.

"Who are you, mister?"

The man looked respectful. "Name's Durant. From Kansas City."

"How come yore ridin' this coach?"

"Goin' to Abilene on business." Durant looked at the gold with wide-open eyes. "Had no idea this coach was carrying gold." He smiled. "Wouldn't have been ridin' on it."

"Whut sorta business you got in Abilene?" asked Burt.

"Cattle business, sir. Hope to buy cattle and ship it."

Burt stared hard at him; the man's blue eyes looked steady and honest.

Burt turned to the woman. She had been jolted by what had happened to the driver and guard, and was leaning against the stagecoach.

"Did ya have to kill 'em to get what you want, mister?" she demanded.

Burt grinned and looked at Joad. A lot of nerve in the filly. She looked like a fine hayride.

"Sorry, miss," Burt said, "but they weren't goin' to hand it over polite. This way we avoid argument and no passenger gets hurt."

"What argument? They're dead."

He smiled. "See? Everything's peaceful. What's the name?"

She glared. "Ruby. Gonna shoot me, too?"

Burt's smile stayed on his face as if it were painted

there. "Naw, Ruby. We don't shoot women, especially pretty ones like you. Better things to do with you than that."

She glanced at Durant, and her lips firmed. "You men are desperados. Not nice at all."

Joad laughed. "You'd be surprised how nice we can be when we meet a nice girl like you."

She stared hard at Burt. "Whut you gonna do with us?"

Burt shrugged. "We're gonna hold the coach for an hour or two, then send it on to Abilene, 'cause folks'll start worryin'. Durant here is gonna ride you there. But for that hour or two, we're goin' to entertain you. How'd you like that, Ruby?" He scooped up a couple of gold pieces. "Reward you handsomely for your time."

Durant's eyes narrowed; he was kneeling next to the stagecoach.

Burt smiled. "Any objections, Durant?"

Durant shook his head. "I never argue with a gun. Bad for the digestion. Don't carry them, either. Try to avoid bloodshed."

Burt nodded. "Nice sense of humor you got. Stand up, will ya?"

"Sure."

Burt looked at Joad, who came behind Durant, reached into his pockets, then went into his shirt and pulled out a Derringer.

Durant smiled. "Just a pea shooter. Keep it for card games. If you'd asked, I'd'a tole you."

There was no smile on Burt's face. *"But you didn't tell me."* He paused and Durant, seeing the gleam in Burt's eyes, figured his time had come. Moving with lightning speed, he grabbed Joad with powerful hands, pulling him between himself and Burt, while his hand seized the gun from Joad's holster. He brought it up to fire, but the bullet from Burt's gun hit his right eye peering from behind Joad, leaving a gaping, bloody hole. His husky body fell slowly to the earth where, after convulsive squirming, he went still.

There was a heavy moment of silence. Ruby brought her arm over her face and turned to the coach.

"A Pinkerton man," said Burt slowly. "Sent along to guard the money."

"When did you know?" Joad demanded, pulling his gun from Durant's stiffening fingers.

"Knew at the sight of him," Burt said.

"Then why in hell didn't you shoot him right off?" Joad demanded. "He coulda killed me. He was strong as a bull."

Burt shook his head. "Didn't want to shock the lady." He looked at her, then turned to the coach. "Hope yore not too upset, Ruby."

At these words, she looked at him, still pale, and bit her lip, determined to get her bearings. "No, I'm not upset. Seen plenty of killin's in my time." She looked down at Durant. "He was a nice man," she said finally. "Had no idea he was there for the money."

Burt motioned to Luke, who picked up the leather pouches and thrust them into the saddle pack on Burt's big black.

Then Burt said, "We're all here for the money, Ruby." He moved toward her. "But that's no reason not to have some fun. Is it?"

6

Burt Dancer looked at the moon sailing in a light blue sky, casting silver light on grass, brush, and boulders. Soft sounds of night animals stealthily hunting prey drifted to his ears. He, Joad, and Luke were sitting in a cove bounded by big boulders, which gave shelter as well as a good sweep of the land. They had finished eating and were sitting around the fire which was burning in a pit. Joad glanced back at Ruby resting on Burt's bedroll next to some thick brush about ten yards away. He spoke in a low, exultant voice. "It's a big haul, Burt. We'll live high on the hog for a time."

"Could be," said Burt. He had a bottle of whiskey nearby, and he poured himself a drink.

"Never can tell," said Luke. "Remember Fort Worth. We had a good grab then, too, and were forced to leave it in Waco."

"A rotten piece o' luck," said Joad. "It was Diggers. Leaving the money pouch in his hotel room while he went down to gamble, and then running hard when the posse rode into town."

"Don't remind me of that," growled Burt.

"What do we do about Diggers?" said Luke.

"What d'ye mean, Luke?" asked Burt.

"Where is he? Can't be counted on. What if we had needed him?"

"Well, we didn't need him. And he's a Dancer. He gets his cut."

Luke shrugged. "I ain't so hot on that, Burt. If a man takes a risk, he gets a cut. That's how I see it."

Burt stared at him coldly. "He's a Dancer, Luke. That's all need be said. Jest like you are." He sipped whiskey, then glanced at the moon. "Don't like it that he's not here. Somethin's wrong. Shoulda been here by now. We hafta find out what happened in the morning."

There was a long silence.

"What about Rafe? Where'n hell is he?" asked Joad.

"Yeah, what stopped him from gettin' to the Pass?" said Luke.

"Figger he's sleepin' off a bad drunk in Ledville?" asked Joad. "He's done it before."

There was another silence, then Luke glanced at Ruby. "What do we do with her, Burt?

Burt grinned. "What d'ya usually do with a good-lookin' filly?" He drank from his cup and passed the bottle to Joad.

"I'm talkin' about after. She's gonna talk, no matter

what. They're gonna ask her what happened to the stagecoach and the money."

Burt shrugged. "What d'ya do? Shoot her? You don't shoot a woman like Ruby. We're already wanted men, Luke. I wouldn't worry 'bout it. We got good horses and good protection." He patted his holster. "We'll move south, mebbe to Mexico, till things cool."

He looked over at Ruby. He craved a woman and he had been thinking hard about her, fascinated by her body. She had a fine pair of breasts and buttocks, and silky-looking flesh. But he figured it would be better not to rush things, especially after the killings at the stagecoach. Killings didn't usually leave a woman in the right mood for games on the bedroll.

During dinner she had acted easy, and he caught her looking at him, the look a woman had when she was thinking hot thoughts. It didn't surprise him to see her still awake, her eyes, even at that distance, glowing in the moonlight. He felt a jump in his Levi's, and decided it was a good time for loving. They had knocked off Ed Brady, the son of a bitch who started the damned feud. They had made a great haul. Now to bed down a sexy lady would make the day perfect.

He looked with hard gray eyes at Luke and Joad. "I aim to take a bit of entertainment with Ruby. You boys get some rest."

Joad stared. "You aim to keep the lady for yourself?"

Burt grinned. "From the look of her, it'd take more than even a man like me to make her happy. So whyn't you boys jest rest, build your strength."

Joad rubbed his chin. "You reckon that filly is gonna be agreeable to our attention?"

Burt smiled. "I reckon. But, jest to make sure, I'll smooth the lady with gold."

Joad and Luke grinned and went to their bedrolls.

Burt picked up the bottle, took a gulp, then pulled four gold pieces from the pouch.

Ruby didn't look surprised when Burt came toward her holding the whiskey in one hand, and the gold in the other. She was lying on her back, which perked up her full breasts. He sat near her.

"Were you talkin' 'bout me, Burt?" she asked.

"Mebbe."

"Can I ask, what are your intentions?"

"Dishonorable." He grinned and poured her whiskey in the cup.

She sat up, took the cup, and sipped it slowly. The moon hit her red hair and pretty features. He could see rouged cheeks and full red lips.

"We were talkin' about you bein' a real sport," Burt said. "We figger you deserve some reward." He dropped four gold pieces on her lap.

She smiled broadly. "Looks like love money."

She lifted her dress to show a well-shaped leg. A small purse bulked in the thigh of her stocking. She pulled it out and dropped the money into it. She left her dress high and reached for the whiskey. After drinking, she said, "Did you know gold makes a woman feel more lovin'?"

"If that's the case, Ruby..." he said, and boldly unbuttoned his Levi's.

She slipped out of her clothing. The moonlight gleamed on the curves of her body, the smoothness of her skin. Her breasts were round, almost heavy, with thick nipples. He caressed her breasts, feeling them silky, then tongued the nipples. He did it for quite a while. She sighed with pleasure.

She lay on her back, he pierced her, and the power of his movements made her groan deep in her throat. He grasped her buttocks, lifting her against him. As his excitement sharpened, he suddenly exploded in her. She jumped, squirming from side to side until her body clenched like a fist. They stayed like that for a time, then their bodies loosened.

Finally Burt withdrew, his passion satiated.

"Let's do it again," she said.

He looked down. "You need it again?"

"Yes, again and again."

He smiled. "Wait."

He took his Levi's, slipped into them, and walked softly to where Joad had stashed his bedroll. Joad's eyes were open, his hands behind his head.

"She wants it again and again," Burt said.

Joad grinned. "Hard woman to satisfy?"

"Could be," Burt said softly. "Give her a couple of gold pieces. Makes her more loving."

He watched Joad go to Ruby, heard the soft murmur of voices.

Burt Dancer walked to his bedroll and lay down for the night, feeling that his flesh was quiet. But his mind was not quiet. He thought about Diggers, and wondered again why he had not turned up at the Pass.

It was almost sundown when Slocum pulled up on the roan and looked at Redstone Pass in the distance where the trail curved toward Abilene. By tomorrow noon, Slocum figured, he and Ellie Mae would reach the Pass, then, he hoped, catch up with the Dancers in Abilene.

Now they would camp for the night near this small stream where the horses could drink. A cliff nearby offered a haven and a good campsite.

"We'll camp here, Ellie Mae. By tomorrow sundown, I figure, we'll be mighty close to Abilene. Let's hope that's where the Dancers are going to lay over."

She stared ahead to the Pass, and seemed disgruntled at the idea of stopping. "Any chance of making the Pass before we camp?"

"Couldn't make it before sundown. Won't get a spot good as this. The horses need rest, water, and food. We got water and good cover here."

She nodded and slipped off the saddle. In sheer fatigue, she threw herself on a grassy patch and stretched. Her breasts pulled against her blue shirt. Slocum clamped his jaw, swung off the roan, and opened his saddle pack.

"Wouldn't mind a touch of whiskey," she said, "to ease the aches."

He grinned. "Good idea." He brought out the bottle and poured whiskey in two cups.

She drank some, looking at the sky flaming with primrose, red, and orange. "A Texas sunset," she said. "The best there is."

He looked at the sky. "Not bad."

She perked. "Not bad! You got no soul, Slocum. Ever see anything better?"

He looked broodingly into his cup. "Seen some mighty fine sunsets in Georgia."

Her eyebrows lifted. "So, you're a Georgia man? Shoulda figured that." She looked at the sky, then the land. "We got time to kill, Slocum. Tell me something 'bout yourself. What'd you do in the War?"

Slocum leaned on his elbow, his face grim. The War —he didn't like thinking about it that much. The memory of bullets flying, the suicidal charges. He thought of his own job, sharpshooting the Union officers. There were times in his dreams when he smelled the smoke, heard the roar of the cannon, the groaning of wounded men, the death cries of friends. No, he didn't care much for those days.

"It was a miserable war," he said. "Like wars always are. After it was over, I went back to a piece of land my family had in Calhoun County. Some carpetbagger tried to take it. I didn't like that, and took care of him." He sighed. "Can't go back to Calhoun County any more." He lifted his cup and sipped the liquor. "That's how it was with me."

He looked at her. There was a strange look in her dark blue eyes.

"Why are you looking at me like that?"

She shrugged. "I'm thinkin' you're not an easy man to know. Deep as a well. And quick as a flash with a gun. I'm mighty lucky to have you on my side."

He smiled grimly. "I figure I'm on the right side." He lit a cigarillo. "What about you? What in hell started this feud? Heard that your dad shot old Dancer. How'd it happen?"

"I thought Dad told you." She looked to the distance at the Redstone Pass, then at Slocum. "In the old days, the Bradys and Dancers were good friends. I think my father courted Martha Jane Davis before she became a Dancer. To hear Dad tell it, he and she shoulda married instead. But father got lost on a cattle drive to Kansas City, and when he finally got back, Martha Jane had already married Clem Dancer. Dad was in a fury. To hear him tell it, she was the only woman he ever loved. Anyway, he did marry Lula Jones, and she got thrown by a horse, and died from concussion.

"The boys were small. Me, too. We played with the Dancer kids a lot. Martha Jane would come over, be like a mother to us Bradys, and we loved her. It was easy to see that Dad loved her, too."

Ellie Mae stopped, held her cup out to him. "Pour a little more of that whiskey, Slocum. Well," she went on, "even I could tell that Martha Jane cared about Dad, too. I mean a lot. Clem Dancer picked that up, and he always had a dark hate for father." She grimaced. "One night he was playing cards with Dad, and something was said that made Clem flare up in a terrible jealousy. He raved, said he had reason to believe the worst of Dad. Told Dad to pull his gun right off or he'd shoot his head off."

Ellie Mae stopped, sipped from her cup. "Dad did pull his gun, and that finished Clem Dancer. A fair fight.

"But the Dancers didn't care to hear that. Their father had been shot, and Ed Brady did it. The Dancers are a hard lot, not the kind that forgives. They began to pick off my brothers, my kin. Slowly. The feud went on for a long time. The Dancers were in no hurry. Every so often they'd corner one of the family, and we'd lose a Brady. We tried to defend ourselves. We called in our kin, got some of them. But the Dancers were clever. It was Burt, Bad Burt—he was the schemer. Then the Dancers lost their stock and went bad. I mean, they began to rob and kill. In some towns, they're wanted men. That's why they decided to finish us off. That's why they laid for Dad and Tim. Didn't want to leave the job unfinished. Owed it to their father, I s'pose they'd say. I understand them. I played with them enough. Dad figured they were leaving the territory, goin' elsewhere. Maybe California, Mexico."

She drank off her whiskey, gazed at the sky. Her lovely face looked bitter. "And so they've wiped out my family, my brothers. Finally, my father. But there's still Dancers breathin'—Burt, Joad, and Luke. The only Brady left is me—a woman." She put her hand on her gunbelt. "But I don't have to be strong. Just clever. Just be in the right place at the right time with my rifle." She looked at him, her eyes dark and liquid. "I may not be lucky, but I've got you on my side." She smiled. "That makes me feel good, Slocum."

She looked so appealing that he felt a strong yearning to put his arm around her, to give her comfort. But he stifled the urge. The girl had just told a terrible story of how she'd lost her entire family to the guns of the Dancers. She might misunderstand his gesture. He thought of the Dancers, and his eyes gleamed. "We'll catch up sooner or later, Ellie Mae. Maybe in Abilene. Wherever the trail leads."

Her face set hard. She put down the cup of whiskey and looked at the great mountain ranges soaring west. She seemed deep in thought.

Finally, she spoke in a harsh voice. "Keep in mind, Slocum, that Burt Dancer is foxy. He knows me, and he figgers the Dancers are never gonna be safe long as I'm breathin'. Given the chance, he won't hesitate to mow me down. So he won't just keep running. Running is not Burt's style. He's the kind of cowboy who would reverse his tracks and come after us. He's seen us kill Seth. He'll be missing Diggers, want to know what happened. He may even learn about Rafe. So it's smarter not to think that we're gonna catch him, but that he's gonna catch us."

They got a fire going and fried a rabbit that Slocum had shot earlier in the day. This time Ellie Mae ate with relish. Hard riding over miles in the hot sun had left her with a hearty appetite.

While Slocum ate, he couldn't help thinking about Ellie Mae. Smart as a fox. She had worked out the strategy of her enemy. You could do her kind of thinking if you knew what made a man like Burt tick. Would he truly shoot a woman like Ellie Mae, a girl he'd known all his life? She thought so. He knew she was after his hide, and would never rest till she got it. But would he come after her, shoot her, so that he and his clan could sleep nights? Or would he just lose himself in the territory so that she would give up hunting the Dancers?

7

Slocum looked at the peaks of the mountain, now fired by the flames of the sunset. The pikes of stone glittered like spears thrust upward, weapons looking for victims.

It was then that, to Slocum's amazement, he heard a familiar voice behind him.

"Don't move or I'll put a bullet up your ass, Slocum. You, too, purty lady."

It was Beaks, and the moment he heard the voice, Slocum cursed himself for his dumbness, letting a mangy dog like Beaks live. Now the fat was in the fire. How in hell did he get here, and behind him?

"Now," said Beaks, "both of you pull yore guns— the handle, with yore fingers. No tricks, Slocum, or I shoot. Yore dead, anyway, I'm jest gonna give yuh a little time. So, pull the guns carefully and toss 'em behind you."

Slocum ground his teeth in rage. Glancing at Ellie Mae, he saw her pale face as she tried desperately to think of something. His jaw hard, he nodded at her. Every moment they had to live offered a moment for Beaks to make a mistake; a wrong move now could be fatal.

With his fingers he lifted his gun and dropped it. "Do it, Ellie Mae."

She let out a deep breath as she dropped hers. There was despair in her mind: she'd been thinking all the time of the Dancers and sweet revenge, but here came this polecat from nowhere to put a stop to everything. Why, oh, why did Slocum let this rotten dog live?

"Move off just a piece." Beaks, grinning, crept forward, lifted the guns, and shoved them in his gunbelt. Slocum looked at him, at his narrow face with its sharp nose, dark eyes, and malevolent grin.

"Slocum," he said, "I been lookin' to this moment a long time."

Slocum's green eyes looked piercingly at the scruffy man in front of him. "Don't know why, Beaks. I gave you your life. Don't know why you'd come back."

Beak's face distorted with cruelty. "You dunno whut you did, Slocum. You killed Blake. Only friend I had in this world. We been mates for years. You shot him and now I got nobody."

He stopped, pulled a cigar from his chest pocket, and lit it casually, enjoying his power as he held the gun on them.

"Where'd you get the gun, Beaks?" Slocum asked, though he had a good idea.

Beaks grinned. "Went to where Blakie was buried, where you threw the gun. Pretty smart, hey, cowboy?" He sat on a rock nearby and smoked, staring at Slocum.

"I'm gonna tell you what happened. Figure yore interested. I did start for Ledville. Traveled a time, broodin' about Blakie. Lost my best friend. It's the worst feelin' a man can have. More I thought 'bout it, the more it hurt. Hadda do somethin' for ole Blakie."

Ellie Mae watched Beaks with disgusted fascination. The last thing she wanted was for this worm of a man to block her pursuit of the Dancers, her deadly enemies. Yet he had done it, and he could do a lot worse. She glanced at Slocum, standing easy, his green eyes fixed hard on Beaks.

"Sit down, will ya." Beaks pointed with his gun to the rocks nearby. "I got a lot on my mind, don't mind talkin'. For a time," he finished grimly.

He puffed on his cigar and watched them perch on two rocks. "Ya see, Slocum, I decided to do for Blake what he could no longer do. That'd be the only way to fix it for him. And whut did he want?"

He grinned fiendishly, looking at Ellie Mae, then Slocum. He tapped his cigar. "So there I was headed for Ledville, thinkin' bad thoughts. Whut d'ya s'pose stopped and turned me around?"

"Got no idea," Slocum said, hard-faced. Beaks was crazy for revenge. He had the drop and Slocum could think of nothing to do.

"I'll tell ya. Hey, Soft Cloud—come out!"

Slocum turned toward the cliff and saw the Indian maid, in her buckskins and moccasins, come from behind a boulder. She walked proudly, her glowing dark eyes staring at Slocum.

Beaks was grinning. "Here came this pretty squaw, riding alone right at me, not seeing me till it was too late, o' course. I fired a bullet in front of her and she stopped. Soft Cloud. I figured my luck had changed. So I gave her my best compliments." He grinned evilly. "She's fine piece o' woman, Slocum. Too bad you'll never know."

Slocum had been wondering how Beaks had reached this campsite so quietly, and now he had an idea. "I gotta say, Beaks, you did great tracking to get here, and me not noticing. How'd you do it?"

"Couldn't do it in a year. But *she* did it. She helped. Don't know why. Mebbe she figured you'd help her out. Fat chance. She was the one who brought me to this campin' site, working the trail to get in front of you. Sundown was comin', and she figured you'd pick this spot, and we'd be waitin'." He puffed at his cigar, looking pleased. "So whaddya think of all that?"

Slocum was thinking that as long as Beaks talked, he wasn't shooting, and that was good.

"I reckoned you to be a mighty clever cowboy, getting in front of me, Beaks. But the Indian girl did it, not you. So I have to admit you ain't that clever after all."

Ellie Mae jumped in. "Listen, Beaks. Slocum gave you a decent break—to go on to Ledville and live. Can't think of many men who woulda done that. Most would have shot your butt off. So whyn't you do the right thing? Let us go our ways. We got no quarrel with you." She stood up, as if the matter was settled.

His eyes glittered crazily. Slowly he raised his gun, fired a bullet that whistled past her ear, then swung the gun at Slocum, who had been ready to spring at him.

He grinned, looking from one to the other. "I coulda

shot you to pieces, purty lady, but I ain't stupid enough to kill a woman. Like you, specially. You got a fine body, and I aim to enjoy it. This brown-skinned squaw ain't exactly my taste."

He glanced at the sky, where the sun was perched on the horizon. Then he studied Slocum, and his face twisted with fury. "Jest 'cause I'm talkin' don't mean I don't have a *hate* on you, Slocum. You did the most rotten thing in the world when you shot Blakie."

He walked a step closer to Slocum. "And now I'm tellin' you what I'm gonna do. I know you're achin' to know. Gonna tie you up to that rock and leave you there for the buzzards." He grinned diabolically. "They gotta eat, too. And I save a bullet.'

Ellie Mae's face contorted with horror. "You gotta be the lowest creature that ever walked like a man," she said.

He stared at her, and his expression became vicious. "Rave on, little lady. I'll pay you off later. Got some funny tricks. It's gonna be lots of fun. After we get rid of him." Keeping his gun ready, he took a cut piece of rope curled around his gunbelt, and threw it at the Indian girl.

"Tie him, Soft Cloud." He put his wrists together to show her.

She scowled, but did not move to the rope.

Beaks fired a bullet at her feet.

She picked up the rope and, moving to Slocum, her black eyes gleaming, got in front of him.

"Don't try tricks, Slocum," Beaks said suddenly, "or I'll shoot the girl, then you." He grinned. "I won't kill you. Hit a piece of you. Got a lot of hungry coyotes out here need feedin'."

The Indian girl turned to look at Beaks, then threw down the rope and faced him.

He was astonished. "What the hell's the matter with you? Tie him, I said."

She stood immovable.

His jaw hardened. "All right, you dirty redskin. Don't need you any more. You did your job. Now you're in the way."

He raised his gun to shoot her. There was a soft, swishing sound as an arrow catapulted through the air, striking Beaks in the neck with such force its steel tip came through the flesh of the other side.

His face distorted, he gasped for air, and choked, spewing blood, falling to the ground as his hand clawed frantically at the arrow, trying to pull it out.

Moving with lightning speed, Slocum grabbed the gun dropped from Beaks's lifeless hand, and in a crouch studied the cliff.

The squaw held up her hands, one to Slocum, the other to the Indian still hidden in the rocks.

"Not to shoot!" she shouted in English. Then she repeated it in her own dialect. She stopped to listen, but no sound came from the Indian crouched among the rocks. She spoke again, her voice rising with passion. To Slocum, she seemed to be explaining. Then she stopped.

A voice came from the rocks, then the Indian seemed to materialize. He had a broad, high-cheeked face, coal-black hair, and black eyes that looked at Slocum without fear. He had a muscular torso and strong legs. He held the bow in his hand, and a quiver of arrows was strung behind him. He never took his eyes off Slocum as he came forward.

"I am called Soft Cloud," the girl said to Slocum. "Red Sun knows you are a friend. You saved me from disgrace by the wolves, one of whom lies there."

Slocum looked at Ellie Mae in wonder, then turned to the girl. She knew the language, she had finely cut features. Probably a white mother, an Indian father.

He spoke slowly. "Tell Red Sun that his skill with the arrow is great, and that Slocum and his squaw give thanks. Slocum owes his life to Red Sun."

Soft Cloud looked at Ellie Mae, and a small smile appeared on her lips as she read the look on the lady's face, hearing herself called "squaw."

She turned to the brave who came forward, the muscles of his powerful thighs rippling. He listened to Soft Cloud translating Slocum's words. When she had finished, Red Sun bowed his head, his face solemn.

Soft Cloud then sat down cross-legged on the ground, and Red Sun came to her and ran his hand softly over her black hair, a look of tenderness in his eyes.

Ellie Mae, watching, seemed to be touched. "It has to be love, Slocum," she said in a low voice.

Slocum shrugged. "Might be his sister. Her mate was killed by Beaks's bunch, you may remember."

Soft Cloud had acute hearing. "He is the brother of my mate," she said. "Red Sun has followed the steps of Soft Cloud for many moons, seeking revenge for the death of his brother. His arrow has found its home."

Now the brave stared piercingly into Slocum's eyes and spoke quickly to the girl.

She turned to Slocum, her face serious, her head high. "Red Sun says he understands what you have done for Soft Cloud. He offers to be your blood brother."

Slocum was moved by the sincere, almost noble look of the Indian. "Say that Slocum gladly takes the honor to be blood brother to Red Sun."

After the translation, Red Sun put his right hand to his heart, a gesture that Slocum repeated.

A bit later, Slocum and Ellie Mae watched the two Indians move up the rocky incline to their horses.

The moon was climbing in the sky when Slocum, shovel in hand, looked down at Beaks.

"He meant to leave me for the coyotes. Why can't I do as much for him?"

"'Cause you're not a buzzard like him," Ellie Mae said.

Later, she gazed at the silver moon high in the sky, casting deep shadows on the mountain ranges in the distance.

"Tomorrow, Slocum, we go after the meanest buzzard of them all . . . Burt Dancer."

8

Burt Dancer was thinking hard as he watched the rising sun. Joad and Luke, drinking their morning coffee, watched Burt. Finally Burt, who had been smoking a cigarillo, flipped it into the air.

"We gotta find out 'bout Diggers once for all," he said to Luke. "Me and Joad will ride through Abilene to the hideout house and bury the gold in the ole hiding place. Meanwhile, Luke, you ride to find out about Diggers. Track back and be careful. Look for hostile Injuns, look for Ellie Mae and her big cowboy. Could be they did mischief to Diggers." Burt's jaw clenched.

Joad scowled. "No reason to think that about Diggers. It's expectin' the worst, Burt."

"He's twenty-four hours late. Figger it's got to be serious. Luke, you *find* Diggers. Make sure. Don't want smart guesses. We want to know what happened." His gray eyes had a steely glint.

Luke nodded. "Where do we meet?" he asked.

"After me and Joad go to the hideout house, we'll come back to Abilene. Meet at the saloon." He glanced at Ruby, who was combing her hair near a boulder. She smiled at him.

Burt turned back to Luke, his face hard. "Be smart. Be careful. You better ride now."

"I'll find him, Burt." Luke's lips were pressed thin. "Wherever he is."

He walked to his pinto, tightened the cinches, and swung over the saddle. They watched him. He looked at them, then at Ruby, who gave him a broad smile.

The sun crept slowly upward as Luke backtracked the trail left by the Dancers when they rode west. His face was set hard and his body ached from the strain of staying taut. He approached open land carefully, tried to stay behind rock and brush, and studied what lay in front of him. Only when he felt confident did he move.

He saw a mountain lion, a herd of elk, eagles, hawks, and buzzards, but no Diggers. Once he saw two Indians riding north, a brave and a squaw, and wondered if she was the girl who had been with Diggers. His jaw hardened, but he had to stay with the tracks.

By noon, when the sun hit the earth hard, he caught sight of two more riders. They were tracking, and it was clear to Luke who they had in mind. Ellie Mae and her big cowboy were working the Dancer trail. Luke's position was north of the trail, fairly safe if he stayed put. For a moment he thought of chancing a long rifle shot to pick off the cowboy, but he remembered Burt's orders: find out what happened to Diggers. What if he missed his shot? There would be gunfire; anything could happen. Better let them pass and do his job. There would be time later for the showdown. He stayed hidden and watched them ride west.

A stab of anxiety went through Luke as he kept backtracking, thinking about Ellie Mae. He had known her since they were yearlings. In fact, she had been his first secret love. Once he had had a hidden desire of marrying up with her, and he thought most of the Dancer boys had probably played with that idea. All that was before the feud, of course.

Luke had come to live with the Dancers when his own parents had been killed by Apaches. He thought himself part of the Dancer family. When old Brady killed his uncle Clem, everything went poisonous. Luke had to draw his gun against the young Bradys, boys he had played with. Now he was forced to think of Ellie Mae as the enemy. She could shoot like a man, and she'd just lost her brothers and father. There was plenty of steel in that filly. Luke felt she could shoot a Dancer without drawing an extra breath.

He had to keep that fixed in his mind. They might have been playmates once, but she would just as soon kill him as kiss him now. Burt had said it, and Burt was smart. He always figured the easy way, never stampeded, kept a cool head. Burt had said, "Be careful with Ellie Mae, she can sting like a rattlesnake."

It was mid-afternoon when Luke found the freshly dug grave. His heart missed a beat. *Damn!* He looked at the land nearby, a pileup of rocks to the north. A man could ambush from there. Was that what had happened?

Someone had been killed and buried. Not an Indian.
This was a white man's grave. Luke approached the
mound, his nerves tingling. Burt wanted to know. That
meant he would have to dig. Grim-faced, he pulled his
shovel from his saddle pack and dug quickly, his face
sweating, his heart beating hard, until he uncovered a
piece of Levi's.

Luke stopped and his jaw hardened. Diggers! He
knew those Levi's. With his fingers he scooped the dirt
away from the face.

Diggers's eyes were closed, his face covered with
dirt. He looked like he was sleeping. Sleeping the long
sleep.

Luke went to his saddle pack, pulled out his whiskey
bottle, and took a deep drink. He wiped his mouth, took
another. Diggers was almost a brother to him.

What the hell, it was over for him. How did he get
it? Burt would want to know. Carefully he scooped the
dirt away from the body until he saw the wound. Rifle
bullet. He'd been backshot with a rifle.

The shot came from those rocks, just as he had figured. Who did it? He studied the tracks. Moccasins—
the Indian girl, the cowboy, and Ellie Mae had all been
here.

He took another long pull from the whiskey bottle
and wiped his brow.

It would be rotten news to Burt and Joad. Burt already sensed it. Still, it would hit them hard. Diggers
had been a hard case who just liked the ladies too much.
It did him in. He stopped for the Indian girl, had to have
her. Well, that was that.

Luke mounted up, his jaw set hard. What should he

do? Catch up with Ellie Mae and the cowboy. What then? Could he shoot Ellie Mae? He bit his lip. He didn't know the answer to that. He would face it if he had to.

But first he had to tell Burt and Joad that their brother, Diggers, was dead.

As Luke rode west, he thought of Ellie Mae. She'd shot Diggers, hadn't she? It had to be her. He'd seen the prints coming from the rocks. So his honey girl, Ellie Mae, had killed ole Diggers.

Luke bit his lip so hard he could taste blood.

The sun burned fiercely on the land as Luke pushed his pinto. He no longer bothered with tracking, but rode by landmarks. It was almost sundown when he picked up the fresh tracks of Slocum and Ellie Mae. From there on he moved cautiously on a trail that climbed precipitously into rocky, convoluted trails. When finally he reached the peak and peered down over a jutting rock, he caught sight of Ellie Mae and her cowboy moving slowly along a narrow, rocky ledge.

Now that he had them in sight, Luke felt he could ease up. He had been fearful that he might be running the pinto into lameness, but now he could stop to let the horse rest and drink. Luke ate strips of beef jerky washed down with whiskey. Then he swung over the horse and followed the tracks cautiously. When he saw them again they had stopped to eat.

He considered again whether to take a potshot at Slocum, and decided not to. He had to bring back the news of Diggers to Burt.

He tied the pinto to a branch and climbed to get into a position to observe Ellie Mae and Slocum.

Watching them, Luke saw their horses neigh and pull frantically on their reins. From his vantage point, he caught sight of a crouching mountain lion, crawling to attack one of the horses. Slocum grabbed his rifle. The lion slithered swiftly into a thicket of bushes and was gone. Slocum yelled at Ellie Mae and started to track the lion. For a time Luke watched Slocum tracking. He disappeared into the high thicket. It gave Luke a fine opportunity. He moved fast and silently.

Ellie Mae had comforted the horses and gone back to the fire to wait for Slocum.

Silent as a panther, Luke moved near Ellie Mae. She sensed his presence and stiffened, her hand going to her gun.

"Don't move, Ellie Mae."

She cursed softly under her breath. "Luke?"

He walked in front of her. "Drop the gun, Ellie Mae."

They stared at each other for a long moment. "Gonna shoot me, Luke?"

He bit his lip. "I wouldn't want to do that, Ellie Mae. But if you force me, I just may. Drop your gun on the ground, that's all."

She did it.

"What the hell are you doing here, Luke?" she asked.

He stared at her hard. "Lookin' for Diggers."

She gazed at him silently.

"Mebbe you've seen him?" he asked.

"Mebbe *you* have," she said, hard-faced.

"I seen him," he admitted, his teeth gritted.

"You Dancers killed my father," she said in a flat voice.

"There's been a lot of killin's, Ellie Mae." He looked toward the thicket. "Don't have much time. Now tell me—who's the cowboy with you? What's he doin' with you? Is he your kin, from far off?"

"His name's Slocum. No kin."

"Did he shoot Diggers?" he asked.

She turned away.

Luke bit his thumb. "Slocum's a dead man. But I'd hate to see something happen to you, Ellie Mae. I'm here to warn you: Stay away from Abilene. Stay away from the Dancers. The last thing we . . . I . . . want is to hurt you. We all loved you once. You were our favorite honey girl. And I'm sorry we've given you pain. But you have to understand—this crazy feud—we didn't start it. I'm warning you again. Stop tracking us and stay away from Abilene. We Dancers know you, what you would do. Burt doesn't trust you farther than he can kick a horse."

She stared at him coldly. "You Dancers killed my father. Tim is dead, too."

Tim! Luke scowled. How could she know that? They had picked up Brady and her on the trail. How could she get such news? Slocum . . . did he bring it?

"Who told you about Tim?"

Her blue eyes glowed. "Rafe is dead, Luke. You see, it ain't just the Bradys who are dyin'."

Luke looked jolted. A deep wave of sorrow went over him. In the last two days they had lost Seth, Rafe, and Diggers. His cousins—more like brothers to him.

"What happened to Rafe?" His voice was hoarse.

"Slocum shot him in Ledville. Rafe was cardsharpin'."

Luke looked off in the distance. No sign of Slocum. Still trying to smoke out the lion, probably.

Then he looked at Ellie Mae. Such a cute filly; he still had the old feeling for her. He didn't want her hurt.

"Listen, Ellie Mae, the times are bad. All this killin' will do wild things to Burt. Better for you to get away. Go to your kin, John Brady in Paso. Start life there. And forget this cowboy, Slocum. He's a dead man. That's my advice."

He stepped forward, picked up her gun, threw it, and backed away. "You were the apple of my eye, Ellie Mae. Maybe after this is settled we could get together. You sho' got my heart. Now I'm off to Abilene. Don't be stupid. Don't follow. Would hate to see *you* join all the other Bradys."

The ears of Slocum's roan, tied near a thicket, suddenly went up. The sound of the padded claw had been soft, but the horse could smell it, and it had the scent of death. A primordial instinct set off the alarm. Neighing loudly, the roan jerked hard at the reins holding him. Slocum, who had been sitting with Ellie Mae, grabbed his rifle and sprang to his feet. It was the movement of the man that saved the horse from the mountain lion crouched to attack. For an instant, the lion froze; then it slithered into the thicket.

"Watch the horses!" Slocum yelled to Ellie Mae, and he started after the lion. It was sundown, and they had staked their campsite. He didn't want this mountain lion prowling around it all night.

Slocum had barely glimpsed the brown, bullet-shaped body as it slouched into the thicket. He didn't want to tackle the lion. In fact, he admired its grace and strength, but there could be no rest with a lion prowling the campsite. Moving deeper into the growth of brush, Slocum studied the claw marks on the ground. Curious, he thought, how the lion hated man, yet feared him. Was it an instinctive fear of man or of his weapons? Deep in the shadowy brush, Slocum peered ahead. Suddenly indecisive, he stopped. He had lost the tracks and he didn't know which way to move.

In the thicket, the lion crouched on a tree trunk, its yellow eyes glittering venomously as they watched the man, the hated enemy, move stealthily ahead, then stop. He was a big lion who had reached his full growth. That could happen in this dangerous land only through craft and strength. The lion knew when to strike and when not to. He had been hungry, and the smell of horse brought him to the man's camp. Only the smell of the man had made him hesitate. The big cat's yellow eyes studied the man, standing near, his green eyes searching. Crouching, his bullet-like body mobilized to jump, the lion waited for the man to take one more step.

Slocum held his breath, some deep instinct warning him of danger, though it was hard to see in this tangled, shadowy thicket. He strained his ears, but could hear nothing. Silently he lifted his foot to move a step forward, when he heard the soft sound. His instincts screamed. Before he could think what to do, his gun came up firing, the bullets crashing into the sleek, muscular body hurtling at him through the air.

The lion jumped as the bullets tore his body, twisting in anguish. He fell, squirming, but even as he fell, his claw tore at the man. Then the lion died.

The sun was down below the horizon when Ellie Mae, who was sitting at the fire thinking about Luke Dancer, saw Slocum come out of the thicket. He looked pale; his shirt was wrapped around his left forearm.

Ellie Mae stood up, her lips tight.

Slocum smiled. "I got the cat, but he left his mark on my arm."

She went quickly to his saddle pack, pulled out some cloths and his bottle of whiskey. He sat at the fire and looked at his arm. Well, he had scars from knife and bullet; now he had the scars of a lion.

When she brought the whiskey, he poured some over the bloody claw marks, then took a long gulp. Ellie Mae tied the thick cloths around his forearm.

She shook her head. "Not your best idea, tracking the lion."

He shrugged. "Couldn't have that big cat worrying the horses all night. And what if he grabbed one?" Slocum's green eyes stared at her. "Bad deal, being out here with one horse."

She sat next to him, and was jarred by the sudden scowl on his face. His hand moved to his holster.

"What is it, Slocum?"

"Someone seems to have dropped by," he said, pointing to the print of a boot.

"Luke Dancer," she said.

"And where's he now?"

"Gone. He sneaked up, got the drop on me. Said he had been looking for Diggers."

Slocum's face was grim. "Find him?"

"Found him. Dug him up." She looked at the setting sun. "He wanted to know if I shot Diggers. He knew I did it. He didn't want to tell that to Burt."

She smiled. "Luke as a kid was sweet on me. That's why he didn't kill me. He warned me not to go to Abilene."

Slocum shifted the bandage on his arm. The cuts were still bleeding; it was making him feel weak. "And are you going to Abilene?" he asked.

Her jaw hardened. "They killed my father and my brothers. Wherever the Dancers are, that's where I'm going."

He nodded and looked at the mountain peaks against the sky, which had gone mottled gray. "May need a day or two to get my strength back. That cat tore some blood outa me. See how I feel at sunup."

He looked up; three heavy-bellied buzzards were circling in the sky. A pity, he thought. The lion, a magnificent animal without fear, would be devoured by these miserable, craven-hearted vultures.

Dark came down suddenly and big stars began to sparkle in the night sky. Slocum lay easy on his bedroll, listening. The horses were quiet; they had nothing to fear now.

Slocum looked up at the stars. They glowed in a dark, limitless heaven. Low on the horizon, the moon started its silver climb.

Slocum shifted uneasily because of the pain in his arm, thinking how peaceful the stars looked, while on earth everything seemed to be at war. In nature, the main thing was to survive. He thought again of the lion, feared by all animals. Yet, when dead, it just served as fodder for the mangy buzzards.

The buzzards were a bit like the Dancers.

He wondered where they were now.

9

It was late in the afternoon when Luke rode into Abilene. Main Street was clogged with riders, shoppers and their rigs, and some cattle herded through by cowboys.

He stopped at Bridey's Saloon, swung off the pinto, and tied it to the rail. When he pushed the batwing doors, a gush of sound hit him from the men drinking at the bar and playing cards at the tables. It was a big saloon, with upstairs rooms where some of the party ladies entertained.

Luke looked for Burt and Joad, but they weren't there yet. He saw Charley McGrew, the one they called Claws, and two of his boys, Mattie and Tommy. Not the sort of men Luke wanted to meet just now, but they were there, and he could do nothing about it.

Claws was standing between his men at the bar. At the sight of Luke, his face brightened. "Well, look what a bad wind blew in, boys," he said loudly. "One of the Dancer bunch."

Luke put himself at the end of the bar, nodding coldly to Claws. When Bridey, the barman, came over, he said, "Whiskey."

Claws moved to Luke, followed by his two men. "Reckon you don't hear too good, Luke, so I'm here. Would you be in town by yourself? Where's Burt? Bad boy Burt? Been on the lookout for him."

Luke stared at Charley McGrew. He had a round head, a bushy black mustache just over full lips, and dark eyes that seemed to have a sinister glint. His left hand, once chewed by a bear, looked like a claw, which was why he was called Claws. But his right hand was very good, and he pulled a fast gun. Claws had pulled it up and down the territory against reckless cowboys and certain stagecoaches. He was wanted in Kansas and Missouri, which explained why he was in Texas.

Now his black eyes were scrutinizing Luke. "I think I asked you a question, mister. Where's Burt—*Bad Boy* Burt?"

"Dunno just now, Claws. Why'd you want to meet up with him?"

Claws's black eyes shone and his mouth twisted in a mocking smile. "Well, I always like to see his handsome face. But I got a better reason. And if you wanta to hear it, just amble a bit closer."

Luke didn't care to get any closer to Claws than he

had to. "I'm mighty comfortable here, Claws," he told him.

Claws McGraw rubbed his jaw. His mouth had a downward tilt which made him look mean even when he felt mild. Right now he was feeling anything but mild. He glared at Luke, thinking this was one of the Dancer bunch, a fighting, feuding gang. They had been scavenging territory that Claws felt belonged to him. Like just now with the Abilene coach. Claws had scouted the coach and he knew it would be carrying bank gold. The coach never made it to Abilene. In a fury, Claws had sent Mattie Dingus to find out what happened to the coach. He found it all right, but it didn't have a thin dime. All he found was three dead cowboys and a money box shot open. When Claws heard this, he felt as if he had been personally robbed.

Claws knew what had happened to the stagecoach. Only one man in this territory would do a job like that.

"We'll hang around Bridey's," Claws had told Mattie Dingus and Tommy Dawson. Mattie was brawny, scarfaced, and tough. Tommy was a rotund cowboy with a blotchy red face, savage brown eyes, and a quick draw.

"Yeah," said Claws. "Figger that Burt Dancer and his boys pulled this one. Figger he'll show up at Bridey's. We'll wait."

Mattie and Tommy were rowdy boys who liked to drink, and when they did, they shot at anything that displeased them.

Now Claws was studying Luke and smiling.

"Mebbe now that you're here, Luke, Burt will show up. You Dancers stick together like weeds."

Luke looked in the mirror behind the bar, hoping to see Burt come in.

"Did yuh know, Luke," Claws said sardonically, "Burt's been acting extra bad lately."

Luke leaned on the bar, looking casual, and gave Claws a gimlet stare.

"What makes you say that, Claws?"

"What? I'll tell you what." Claws leaned forward, looking mean, but he kept his voice soft. "'Cause there's a stagecoach missing. One coach." He lifted his glass and spoke softly to Luke. "And it was carrying gold." His grin was crooked. "Mebbe *you* know what happened to that coach?"

"No, I don't know." Luke raised his glass.

Claws scowled fiercely. "Whut makes me think you ain't exactly telling the truth?"

Luke looked innocent. "Don't know."

Claws glanced at Mattie, who grinned, showing big yellow teeth. His broad scarred face looked wrecked by barroom fights. "Mattie, what d'ya think? Ole Luke doesn't know whut happened to the stagecoach. Mebbe you oughta refresh his memory."

"I went lookin', Luke. And all I found," said Mattie, "was some dead men and a broken chest. Empty. Jest wonder who would do such a rotten thing?"

"I wonder," said Luke, toying with his glass.

"You got a good sense of humor," said Claws. "I'm gonna ask you again. Where's Burt? You Dancers stick together. But here yore alone. Now it'd be smart to tell me where Burt is."

"Are you gonna pull yore gun if I don't tell ya?" Luke mocked.

Claws's eyes burned. "Don't tempt me, Luke." He

poured a drink in his glass and gulped it, then wiped his mouth with the back of his hand. "It don't matter. I figger if you're here, Burt's gonna be here, too, bye and bye."

"S'posin' Burt does come. What are you goin' to do?" Luke asked.

Claws grinned, and his eyes looked crafty. "I'll offer him a business proposition—so nobody gets hurt. Not the Dancers, nor my boys. I figger there's enough to go around."

Luke leaned his elbow on the bar and looked at one of the party girls, blond and buxom, who was sitting at a table.

Mattie Dingus, who by that time had guzzled enough booze to trigger his meanest instincts, moved next to Luke. "Tell us, Luke, what ever became of that piece of honey, Ellie Mae, you were so sweet on?"

Luke glared. Could he have seen them together out there near Redstone Pass? No, that seemed impossible.

"If I were you, Mattie, I'd keep a clean mouth when I talk about Ellie Mae."

There was a hard moment. Then Mattie, drunk and reckless, grinned. "Sweet on her, hey, Luke? Don't blame yuh. Must be a lotta fun, tastin' a piece o' honey like Ellie Mae."

Luke's right fist went out like a mule's kick, hitting Mattie's jaw.

Mattie staggered back a few feet but didn't fall. He shook his head, then rushed forward, trying to butt Luke in the gut.

Luke sidestepped and hit Mattie again. It jolted Mattie, but he had an iron jaw. He came back and threw punches at Luke with his big knuckled fists. Luke caught a few of them. They slugged head to head for a time, throwing hard punches at face and body, knocking each other back, but both of them, built big and rugged, could absorb the punishment. Then Luke tripped over a chair, going back, and Mattie threw himself on top of him and pummeled him. The cowboys in the saloon cheered. It was the kind of excitement they craved.

A pistol shot hit the big mirror in back of the bar, shattering it into pieces. The fighters froze, as did everyone else, and turned to look at the doors.

There stood Burt Dancer, two guns in hand. To his side was his brother Joad, who also held two guns.

"Fightin's over, gents," Burt said, his gray eyes steely and hard, but his face, as usual, screwed into a seemingly gentle smile. "Anyone thinkin' otherwise?"

There was complete silence. Then the men around the fighters went to their stools and tables. The fighters got up from the floor and began to mop the dirt and blood off their faces.

Burt came slowly forward, his smile still fixed, his eyes alert. The barman looked at the mirror in anguish.

"Sorry 'bout that, Bridey," said Burt. "Hadda get attention." He put some gold pieces on the bar, then came up to Luke.

"Don't like it, you gettin' into trouble when I'm not around. 'Specially when I'm expectin' news from you. Important news."

"Sorry, Burt, but this stinkin' hyena made insultin' remarks about Ellie Mae."

Burt's lips tightened. "Sho' you didn't mean that, did you, Dingus?"

The yellow eyes in Mattie's face were sullen. "Never meant it. Just joshin'." Once Mattie had seen Burt's left-handed gun in action, and to his mind it was awesome.

"Why don't'cha go clean up then Dingus," Burt said.

"Stay put," said Claws, moving from the back, where he had been huddling, watching the action.

Burt frowned. He stared at the mean-eyed Claws. "And what bad luck brought you into Abilene, Claws McGrew?"

"Same one that brought you in," Claws said, his black eyes glittering in the light of the oil lamps. "Like to palaver with you, Dancer."

"What about?"

Claws lowered his voice. "'Bout a stagecoach."

Burt stared at him, then smiled. "Sure, sure. But lemme talk to Luke for a moment." The smile left his face as he turned to Luke and pulled him to the side of the bar.

"What happened to Diggers?" His voice was harsh.

"He's dead."

Burt's expression did not change, but his eyes became lifeless. Though he had been expecting this, it still hit him like a blow in the gut. Diggers gone, the brother born after him. There had always been a close feeling between him and Diggers. He cursed under his breath.

"Who did it?"

Luke bit his lip. "The cowboy traveling with Ellie Mae. Man called Slocum."

Burt's eyes were steely, and his jaw clenched. Then he turned away, his face unsmiling, and walked to the table where Claws McGrew was waiting. He scarcely looked at Claws, but picked up a bottle of whiskey, put the neck to his lips, took a long pull.

Claws was impatient to talk, and not aware of anything different about Burt. "Listen, Dancer, about that stagecoach. I'm troubled 'bout it not showing up. The bank people, I hear, are real upset about it. Sending for some lawman. Seems like there was a nice piece o' gold in that stagecoach. S'posed to be a secret." He smiled. "Not much of a secret. 'Cause somebody knew. Shot up the wagon and got off with the gold."

Burt was looking at the broken mirror with fogged eyes, but he said nothing.

Claws figured he was getting through, and his stubble-bearded face twisted in a crafty grin. He leaned foward and talked softly.

"Listen, Dancer, I was figgerin' on pickin' off this stagecoach—me and the boys. But some clever varmint beat us to it. The boys feel like we been robbed. But I cooled them. I says, looks like we're goin' to have to settle for second best. We figger we could tell the bank boys about the varmints that did this. That might pay for our trouble. But a smarter idea would be to split what *you* found in that chest. It's quicker, and nobody gets hurt. You jest share. What d'ya think?"

Claws, studying Burt, was puzzled by the faraway look in his gray eyes. It seemed almost like he wasn't listening. He pressed forward. "What d'ya think of my proposition, Dancer?"

Then Burt looked at Claws, his eyes, for the first time, seeming to focus on him. Rage twisted in Burt's face, as if the feelings bottled deep about Diggers had surged to the surface and needed a violent breakout.

He pushed back from the table, stood up, and spoke in a dull voice. "What do I think of it? You got five seconds to live, Claws, that's what I think of it."

Claws's face paled. "Are you crazy, Dancer? Can't we talk this out?"

"You got four seconds." Burt's voice was dead.

Claws's face turned mean, his jaw hardened, and he, too, slowly stood up.

The saloon went silent, as if by instinct people knew a killing was about to happen. The two men faced each other in the classic fighting style, hands down to their holsters, fingers bent, knees crouched. Two men on the verge of death.

They stood frozen for a beat, then both went for their guns. Burt's left hand moved like the strike of an adder, so fast it was a blur. His bullet buried itself in the chest of Claws McGrew. Claws, also fast, was just able to fire his gun, but his bullet hit the wall. Claws fell face down, squirmed, then lay still.

Burt stood still holding his gun, and looked at Mattie and Tommy. They were pale, and showed their hands. "Better get him outa here," Burt said.

They bent down to the body.

Joad and Luke were looking at Burt strangely.

"Why'd you do it?" asked Joad.

Burt looked in the mirror at his reflection. He could scarcely recognize his expression.

"Dunno," he said slowly. "It was Diggers. . . . Guess I had to kill someone."

10

Close together, Burt, Luke, and Joad sat silently at a corner table in Bridey's Saloon.

Burt looked deep in thought. The others sensed his mood and let him be. He was mourning his favorite brother, Diggers. Then Burt shook himself and spoke to Luke, his voice rasping. "I want to know about Diggers. Everything."

Luke tenderly touched his cheek, bruised from his fistfight with Mattie Dingus. "I was riding a couple miles east of the Pass when I spotted this fresh-dug grave. It was him in it, Diggers. He'd been rifleshot in the back. I looked at the prints—Indian girl, Ellie Mae, and the cowboy with them, Slocum." Luke pulled a cigarillo from his pocket. "No kin to the Bradys."

Burt's gray eyes fixed on the table, not seeing it. Luke watched him, not daring to speak.

Burt poured a drink from the bottle and gulped it. "Diggers was a blasted fool, always chasing women. I warned him. Told him, 'They'll put you under, boy.' And he said, 'Can't think of a better way to go.' Blasted fool. If he hadn't stopped for the Indian girl, if he'd stayed with us, he'd be alive now. And in the money."

Luke nodded and filled his glass. He felt jittery, because as yet he hadn't given Burt all the bad news. He wondered if he should hold off telling Burt about Rafe. Two brothers—no, three with Seth—lost in three days. It was bad. But how could he hold off telling a thing like that?

Burt's face was tight. "Can't figger it. Why'd Slocum get into the Brady fight? Put himself against the Dancers. Who is he, anyway?"

"Dunno who he is," said Luke, "but he's tough enough. I can make a guess *why* he got in." Luke looked away, swallowed hard.

Burt waited, scowling. "Well, let's hear it."

Luke rubbed his left eye, which was puffed and darkening. "Reckon he figgered the Dancers would be coming after him anyway."

Burt's face was grim. "Why'd he figger that?"

Luke took a deep breath. "Because he'd already shot Rafe. Shot him in Ledville."

Burt turned to Luke, his face rigid. He stared deep into Luke's eyes, as though he didn't understand. "Rafe?" he said, his voice flat.

Luke nodded. "Rafe's dead."

For a long time Burt was silent. Then a bitter smile twisted his mouth. "I was thinkin' we had cleaned up the Bradys, that the feud was over. But it isn't. We've lost Seth, Diggers, and Rafe. Our boys. Our blood. Gone—all of them."

He looked at Joad, then Luke, his fist tightening until it went white. "And it all started with this Slocum. He's the worst thing that's happened to the Dancers. Three of us gone because of him." His teeth gritted. "And this Slocum's traveling with Ellie Mae." He glared at the other two. *"She goes down.* That's what I say. We go after Slocum and kill him *bad. And* Ellie Mae. I know how you feel 'bout her, Luke, but she's part of it. She brought Slocum into this."

Luke's eyes were unblinking. "She lost her father," he said.

"Time she did," Burt said viciously. "He started it. He did the first killing."

"She lost Tim, too," Luke said.

Burt's head jerked forward. "Tim? So we finally got Tim? Rafe did it, right? How'd you learn this?"

"Ellie Mae tole me. Rafe shot Tim, forced a fight."

Burt pulled a cigarillo from his shirt pocket and lit it. "So, they lost old man Brady and Tim. We lost Seth, Diggers, and Rafe. And I thought we were finished with the feud. But Ellie Mae keeps coming. And with her Slocum."

Joad looked curiously at Burt. "This Slocum looks smart and fast."

Luke shook his head. "But he'll never beat the left-handed gun."

"I promise you that." Burt's voice was solemn. "What bothers me is, should we go after him or wait?

Knowing Ellie Mae, I'm sure she'll keep comin'. Won't stop till the end. That's how she is." He turned, his face suddenly fierce. "It means we're gonna have to stop her, Luke. You hear me?"

Luke said nothing.

Burt turned to Joad. "What do you think?

"Maybe we won't have to, Burt. I keep thinkin' of her as a curly-haired kid, ridin' her pony over the range with us kids."

"Them days are gone, Joadie. She's grown up and she's killin'. We gotta forget the ole days."

The gray eyes in Joad's broad face gleamed. "Maybe we can persuade her to go south to her kin, John Brady."

"There's no way you can persuade her. She's stubborn as a mule." He paused, grim-faced. "First thing, let's get Slocum. I want him in the worst way. We'll work out a plan. Don't want to misfire."

Slocum and Ellie Mae, sitting on their horses on the sun-baked slope, looked at Redstone Pass still in the distance. They started toward it slowly because Slocum, clawed by the lion, had suffered a goodly loss of blood, which left him dragging.

"We'll catch up with the Dancers," Ellie Mae had said, "but it'd be best if you felt better when it happens." She couldn't help being miffed about their slowdown and what she felt was Slocum's bad judgment, tangling with the lion.

"Real waste going after that lion," she said when they stopped to rest because the jolt of riding started him bleeding. "Now you're hurt, and we're draggin'. If the Dancers had shot a piece outa you, all right, that couldn't be helped. But to get mowed down by an animal—that wasn't smart."

He scowled. "That lion was after horsemeat. S'pose he got your horse? You mighta had a hard time getting to Abilene, or anywhere else."

She bit her lip. "I'm sorry, Slocum. Guess I'm afeared the Dancers might get away. No reason to believe they're going to hang around Abilene waiting for us."

"Wouldn't worry about it, Ellie Mae. Wherever they go, we'll track them. They won't get away."

Then she did a strange thing. She stroked his cheek with her fingertips and said, "It's nice having you with me, Slocum."

Slocum looked at her delicate face, soft blue eyes, and full breasts. In spite of his blood loss, he felt a quiver of desire. But he stifled the feeling, wondering how long he could hold out before he would try to throw a lasso at her.

They didn't ride much that day or the next. She went hunting with her rifle, and they ate venison, which helped to restore his strength. They talked, and she told him her last kin lived in Paso, her cousin John Brady.

It took two full days before Slocum felt some return of strength. On the morning of the third day, as they jogged toward Redstone Pass, he looked at the vista. The great range of mountains sprawled to the west. A stream meandered lazily south. The sun was bright and glittered off the nearby stone structures poking up from the earth.

When they reached the Pass, Slocum walked to the

rock edge and looked down. There on the trail lay the stagecoach, and he could see the buzzards. He looked grim.

"So that's why the Dancers were in such a hurry," he said.

"What d'ya mean?" she asked.

"Let's go and find out."

The sun was starting down when they neared the stagecoach. Buzzards still clustered around the bodies. "Better wait on that rock," he told her.

He had to fire his gun to jolt the buzzards from their gruesome feast. They had done most of their work; there was nothing recognizable.

Slocum examined the prints, the bullet-blasted locker. He went back to where she sat on a rock, her face tight.

"The Dancers?" she asked grimly.

He nodded. "They were after gold. Reckon that explains why they rushed off after shooting your dad. Wondered why they were in such a hurry. They had to be sure to meet with this stagecoach carrying gold. Shot three men. A woman was here, too. There's another cowboy's set of prints. Someone came to find out what happened to the stagecoach."

She glanced at the buzzards circling overhead, impatient to finish their work. She spoke in a gloomy voice. "It's hard to think I played with the Dancer boys as a kid. I used to think, well, the Dancers are shootin' at us Bradys because they lost their daddy and blame us. But it's worse. They're outlaws—turned into thieves and killers."

Slocum pulled a havana from his shirt pocket and lit

up. The friends of her childhood had become notorious outlaws; it was a bit of a shock to her.

"What'll they do, now that they have the gold? Where will they go?" she asked.

"The tracks looks like Abilene. We'll stay with them."

It was then he saw the lone horseman riding out from behind a big rock pile. He looked big-shouldered, a powerful man in a wide black Stetson, wearing a duster and black boots. He rode a fine, spirited sorrel.

Slocum watched him warily until he saw the star.

The lawman rode close, studying them with narrow eyes, his shooting hand near his holster. "Who are you?" he asked sternly. He had a high-cheekboned face, piercing blue eyes and a bushy mustache that drooped over his lips. His muscles bulged in his clothes.

Slocum didn't particularly care for his attitude, but he answered politely. "Slocum's the name, and this is Ellie Mae Brady."

"Slocum," he repeated. "What Slocum is that? Where from?"

"John Slocum. From Georgia." He wasn't going to say Calhoun County, though there could be no way this sheriff could know what had happened there.

The lawman stared hard at Slocum, as if he could wring out something with staring. Then his light blue eyes swung to Ellie Mae, but her good looks didn't soften him. "And where are you from, miss?"

"North of Ledville. Who are you, mister?"

"Sheriff Wright." He jerked his head at the stagecoach. "Know what happened here?"

Ellie Mae's face was grim. "I'll tell you what happened, Sheriff. The Dancer brothers shot the hell outa the men riding this coach and ran off with the money."

The sheriff's jaw hardened. "How'd you know this?"

"We were tailin' them. That's how we know it."

"And why's that? You tailin' 'em?"

Slocum examined the sheriff; he was beginning to sound either dumb or crafty.

"We got a grudge to settle, that's why," said Ellie Mae, scowling.

The sheriff's blue eyes squinted. "Jest don't get into any fast shootin', miss. There's a lot of money to be accounted for before we do any shootin' or stringin' up." He looked from one to the other. "If things are as you say."

"That's how they are," said Slocum. "Can I ask if you came out to do this by yourself?"

The sheriff offered a thin smile. "Me and this came out to do this." He gently slapped his holster.

"There's three Dancers, sheriff," Ellie Mae said. "And they're killers. Burt Dancer's supposed to be greased lightning."

The sheriff grinned. "Never heard of an outlaw who was not greased lightning, miss. Where yuh headed?"

"Following these tracks. May lead into Abilene."

The sheriff looked at the tracks. "I reckon that's where they're goin'." He rubbed his jaw and stared at Slocum. "Let's see your gun, mister."

Slocum was astonished. "What's that?"

"Your gun. Lemme see it."

"And why would you want that?" Slocum's voice was cold.

"Jest to look at it. Any objections?"

"Plenty. Nobody gets my gun."

The sheriff's jaw was hard. "I'm the law here, mister. I'll ask you again, lemme see your gun."

Slocum gazed at him. He didn't give his gun to anyone, especially a stranger who might not be what he said.

"Nobody gets my gun, Sheriff," Slocum said with an easy smile.

There was a crackling moment of tension. The sheriff's jaws worked hard, and he went for his gun, but found himself staring at the barrel of Slocum's Colt.

Slocum smiled. "Mighta got yourself hurt, Sheriff, if that's who you are. Just keep the gun in the holster and there'll be no trouble."

The sheriff's eyes were wide. He felt he could have been killed. He chewed his lips in frustration, and watched Slocum casually put his gun back in its holster. The sheriff swallowed, then pulled his bandanna off and mopped the sudden sweat on his brow.

"Never had that happen to me," he said slowly. "Who'd you say you were, Billy the Kid?"

"Slocum's the name."

"Mr. Slocum, you had a chance to put me away and didn't. I reckon that proves you honest. And this lady doesn't look like a robber. Sorry I was pushin'. My job is to get the money back for the bank."

"Did you think we shot up the stagecoach, Sheriff?"

"Didn't know, but you were here, and nobody else. Hadda check out who you were." He pulled a plug of tobacco, bit off a piece, and chewed it thoughtfully. "Then your story 'bout these Dancers could be true."

Ellie Mae's lips twisted. "Mighty smart to catch on so fast, Sheriff."

The big man shrugged. "I hear a lotta strange stories

about who did what. Most of them are funny stories. Got so I disbelieve everything until I get real solid proof. Take nobody's word till they're proved out. Now let's ride toward Abilene and find these Dancers."

The sheriff rode out in front of them, as if that was his rightful place. Slocum and Ellie Mae jogged after, talking in low voices.

"Hate to be dependin' on him to protect me from outlaws," Ellie Mae said.

"Can't tell. He might have hidden talents," Slocum said.

Ellie Mae shook her head, looking at the broad back of the sheriff. "He's gonna have to draw faster than that if he hopes to nail Bad Burt Dancer."

"Bad Burt is fast?"

"Fastest ever. The only way I aim to get him is to shoot him when he's lookin' somewhere else."

Slocum shook his head. "Not sportin', Ellie Mae, to fight like that."

"Fight like that?" she repeated, rage gleaming in her eyes. "This ain't a sportin' game, Slocum. Main thing is for the Dancers to be dead. And buried. Just like my folks."

Slocum rubbed the roan's haunches. "You have kin in El Paso, that's right, isn't it?"

"Yes, I have kin there. Cousin John Brady, all that's left of the Bradys."

"Ever think of going there to live out a peaceful life?"

She looked at the land bright in the sun and her eyes misted. "Won't think of it, not so long as there's a Dancer breathing."

* * *

In Bridey's Saloon, Lorrie, the dark-eyed, buxom blonde, watched the three men at the corner table. Two were big and brawny, but it was the third one, the one with the gray eyes, who fascinated her. He was talking intensely, and she sensed his violent feelings. It made her tingle with excitement. She could scarcely take her eyes off Burt Dancer. When he talked, the other two listened carefully.

"The way I see it," Burt was saying, "is that it's smarter to stay here. We keep an eye peeled. They are tailin' us. That means they'll come into town. We'll be waitin', but not where they expect." His grin was cruel. "Ellie Mae can't be thinkin' we're running from her. But Slocum may think that. *He's the one.* We'll take good care of him." He paused, and his jaw clenched with fury as he thought of Slocum. Then his gaze absently flipped over to the blonde who was watching him.

Luke squirmed.

Burt picked it up. "What's botherin' you, Luke?"

"Why don't we just take the money and head for Mexico? Why hang on here? Don't seem smart, hangin' on."

"Yeah," Joad said. "Mebbe we should hit the trail, Burt. Why stay put?"

Burt grimaced. "Nobody knows we hit the stagecoach. Nuthin' to be feared of. I'm thinkin' of Ellie Mae. She'll keep comin' no matter what. She and Slocum. Best to meet them here." He lifted his glass and stared at them. "I know what you're thinkin'. If we make a run, then we won't have to deal with Ellie Mae.

You're thinkin' we'll leave her behind. But she's got Slocum. He's a gun, and he trails like a coyote. We gotta get him, and in the worst way, for what he's done to the Dancers. After that, we'll think what to do with Ellie Mae. But she's a hard case, remember?" He shook his head. "Now, I'm gonna tell you, it's a black time. I feel bad, real bad. We lost our brothers. I can't think of anything that can square that."

He stopped talking. The blonde had stood up slowly and stretched, and her big breasts pushed against her silky blue dress. She slowly walked on shapely legs past Burt's table, looking directly at him. He stared at her dark-eyed, pretty face, her body, then stood up. "See you boys later."

Without a word, the blonde started for the stairs.

Burt followed her as Luke and Joad watched. Then Joad drawled, "Burt gets misery outa his system two ways, with a gun or a woman."

11

As the blonde went up the stairs in front of Burt, he watched the movement of her buttocks. His eye followed the lines of her slender waist as they flowed into her swelling hips.

The room had a bureau, a mirror, a pitcher, a bottle of whiskey, and a bed. Burt grabbed the bottle and took a gulp. He had bad feelings.

She watched him. He wiped his mouth and scowled. "What are you waitin' for?"

She shrugged. "Didn't know you were in such a rip-snortin' hurry. My name is Lorrie." She pulled off her dress. She was big-breasted, with thick pink nipples and rounded hips. And blond all the way, he could tell, looking between her thighs.

"Well, Lorrie, I'm in a hurry," he growled, and flung his clothes off.

She looked at his flesh. "I don't see any fire here."

"No," he growled. "Reckon you're gonna hafta build one."

"Build a fire?" she repeated, gazing at his soft flesh. "And I'd been thinkin' you had a lot of fire burnin' you up."

"I got things on my mind," he said.

She ran a finger over his full lips. "Mebbe you're not in the mood, cowboy."

"I'm in the mood," he growled.

"The way to build a fire." She sank to her knees in front of him and took his softness. He watched her lips moving with professional skill and felt the hardening.

She pulled away, her eyes lit with triumph as she gazed at his rigidness.

His teeth were clenched. "Don't stop."

"Let's try the bed," she said.

There she did more of what he liked, then lay her plump, curvy body on the bed, spreading her shapely legs. He slid over her, felt her warm flesh. He grasped her heavy breasts, held them, then pierced her, plunging to her depths. Without drawing breath, he began to thrust as hard as he could, feeling demon urges, as if by thrusting he could release his pain. He grabbed her buttocks and pummeled, bringing her up to meet his hard thrusts. His tension gathered and he drove into her as if he would nail her to the bed. Then his force exploded and he grabbed her as if he could melt his body into hers. He held her for a time, then let go.

Burt's body felt calm, but in the core of his mind the pain was still there.

He knew it could only be wiped out by one man—Slocum.

Sheriff Wright rode tall and straight in the saddle. He was a proud man who came out of Creek City, where he kept the peace, riding a fast horse and deputizing fast-shooting cowboys. He had been ordered to find out what happened to the Abilene stagecoach and to recover the bank money. He didn't particularly like the idea of traveling too far from Creek City, but his job was to nail lawbreakers. The bank was offering a fat reward for recovery of the gold, and Wright had some ideas about that.

He turned over in his mind what these two riders had told him and tried to piece it together. What in hell were they doing at the stagecoach? How long had they been there? That story about the Dancers . . . did it add up? He'd heard of the Dancers, a feuding family, but he had never heard of them as outlaws. Bad shootup at that stagecoach—three dead. He glanced back at Slocum, riding behind him with the girl. He had never seen a draw like that. It was the first time he ever got beat to the draw. The sheriff wondered if he was slowing down or if Slocum was just lightning-fast. It didn't matter, once they got to town. The woman . . . well, she acted like she was part of the game. Though pretty, she looked like she could handle a gun and could be as hard as nails.

Slocum had seen the sheriff turn. They weren't too far from Abilene, and he was thinking it might be smart to come in after dark, just in case the Dancers had bush-whacking in mind.

He looked at the sinking sun. Not much light left. What would the Dancers do? Run with the money or set a trap for their pursuers? They knew Ellie Mae was on their tail and that he was backing her. That wouldn't frighten them. They also knew by now that they had lost three Dancers: Seth to Ed Brady, Diggers to Ellie Mae, and Rafe to him. But to their minds, it all started when Slocum joined the Bradys. They had to have hard feelings about him. From what he had heard about Burt, he was not a man to run from a fight. More likely, he would wait and play a sly game. Slocum in his time had played a lot of games, but there always could be one he had never played.

He moved the roan up alongside the sheriff. "Might be a good idea to ride in to Abilene after dark, Sheriff."

"Why?"

"The Dancers might try bushwhacking."

"Who?"

Slocum looked at him. This sheriff was turning out to be a prize fool. "We're goin' after the Dancers," Slocum reminded him.

The sheriff turned hard blue eyes on him and looked thoughtful. "Yes, the bloodthirsty Dancers. Well, this is how I'm thinking: Let's say they just robbed the stage-coach. Do you think they're goin' to hang around Abilene, mister? Now, why would they do that? Get themselves caught and strung up. More likely, they're on the run to Mexico. When I get to Abilene, I'll deputize men and we'll track them. We'll head them off."

He smiled indulgently at Slocum. "I've done plenty of trackdowns and I know a thing or two. Jest leave it in my hands, Slocum. I'm glad to have you with me, but this ain't gonna be a fast draw. The way I figger it, we'll trap them on a piece of dead land. Keep one alive, just in case they're not carrying the gold. Most of the time they run with the money." His smile was strange. "Jest leave it in my hands."

Slocum looked at the land around them; it was cluttered with dry brush and stones, a couple of boulders. Serrated rocks climbed high on either side of the trail.

He drifted back to ride alongside Ellie Mae.

"What'd he say?" she asked curiously.

"He wants to go into Abilene *before* dark. Thinks the Dancers are on the run to Mexico with the gold."

She thought about it. "He'd be right if we were dealing with a bunch of outlaws. But these are the Dancers. Burt doesn't run. His gun is fast and he's too proud." She stared ahead. Far in the distance, peeping over the rise, she could see the tops of houses in Abilene.

The sun was down now. Scattered clouds tinged with pink fire filled the sky. "We better make a decision mighty quick, Slocum," she said.

He looked at the sheriff, riding straight and tall toward Abilene. "A real fool," he said.

"Sheriff!" he called. "We'd like you to reconsider. It's our judgment we should hole up till dark, then go in and see what's what in town."

The sheriff partly turned. "I tole you to leave it in my hands. I have experience."

A rifle bullet whined past the sheriff's ear. He flung himself off his horse with ridiculous loss of dignity and crawled fast on his elbows and belly behind the nearest rock. Slocum and Ellie Mae also went flat, finding better cover behind a boulder.

The shot, Slocum figured, came from behind the serrated line of rocks. The Dancers were holed up and waiting. The sheriff's position wasn't good, and a few more bullets skittered around his rock, searching him out. He huddled flat behind the rock and cursed. Slocum and Ellie Mae threw fast fire at the serrated rocks, which did some good. The gunfire at the sheriff stopped.

Nothing was left to do but wait until dark, Slocum thought. It came quickly. Huge black clouds swept over the sky. A long silence from the serrated rocks convinced Slocum the gunmen had backed off. The moon came up and cast a soft light.

The sheriff was in a stew. "Bushwhacking bastards! Who were they?" The glint of suspicion was clear in his eyes.

"Had to be the Dancers," Slocum said.

"Oh, yes, the Dancers," the sheriff said. "They wouldn't be your friends? Why were they shooting only at me?" he demanded.

Slocum shrugged. "A mystery. Maybe you look dangerous. Or you were out front. Or wearing a star."

"Or maybe they were your friends," the sheriff said.

Slocum shook his head. This lawman was dumb enough to start trouble. "Those were the Dancers, Sheriff, come to cut us down before we got to Abilene."

"Cut who down? Didn't you say you were trackin' them? Seems like they'd want to cut you down. So why didn't they? Why were they shooting just at me, cowboy?"

"Have to ask them," Ellie Mae said.

"Seems mighty strange," the sheriff said.

They decided it might be better, after all, to wait a bit before they rode into Abilene.

Ellie Mae came close to Slocum and shook her head. "Can't figure it. Why'd they shoot just at him?"

Slocum grinned. "If you rob a stagecoach, you don't care to have a sheriff around. They saw his star, shiny and bright, and decided to save sheriff trouble later."

"Why didn't they shoot at us?" she demanded. "Don't make sense. Why not shoot you?"

He thought about it. "Maybe they don't want to shoot you yet, just persuade you to leave the territory. As for me, knocking me off at a distance wouldn't be their idea of satisfaction. I figure a man like Burt must be howling mad. They've lost three Dancers since I've joined you. Someone like Burt is not going to be happy just to put a bullet in me at a long distance. Chances are, he'd like to know the bastard who wiped out his brothers, give me a lot of pain. That's why I think nobody shot at me."

"Maybe so." She spoke slowly. Her lips were tight. "If you're right, they'll be waiting for us."

"You were right. You said Burt was not a running man, that he'd try and catch up with us."

"And they're shooting at the sheriff because they can do without him. Best if we protect him," she said.

"Let's go into town. He won't need much protection there."

When they rode into town it was quiet. There were just a few cowboys lounging in front of the hotel. Kerosene lamps threw dim light on the clapboard buildings. The sheriff, looking hard-jawed, pulled up his horse at the bank.

"You folks go ahead. Go to Bridey's. See if you can

find your Dancers. I've got bank business to take care
of."

Slocum looked at him with narrowed eyes. "I'm
thinking it's sheriff business when a stagecoach gets
held up and the desperados are in town."

The sheriff's blue eyes stared at Slocum. "Reckon I
know what the sheriff's business is better than you do,
mister. Right now my business is with the bank people.
I'll get to the desperados at the right time." He swung
off his horse and tied it to the post. "You got a fast
draw, Slocum. Nothing to be feared of. Just go up there,
and if you don't see any desperados, why don't you just
have a whiskey."

Slocum looked at Ellie Mae. She shook her head, but
seemed glad to be free of the sheriff. She felt he might
get between her and the bloody revenge she wanted
from the Dancers.

"Let's go, Slocum," she said in a low voice. "We
don't need anyone."

They trotted their horses down the street to Bridey's
Saloon, a big two-story wooden building with a porch.
Slocum looked at the horses tied to the posts. None
belonged to the Dancers.

"They may not be in there," he said, "but I'll mosey
around. Wait here on the porch."

"No, I'm goin' in, too."

"You're not."

"It wouldn't be smart, Slocum, for you to go in
alone. If they are there, it'll be three guns against you.
You need my gun."

He smiled. "Three of them are not goin' to shoot at
one man, not in front of folks."

"They killed three men on the stagecoach."

"Nobody was watching. We're in town now. Tell you what, if I see them, I'll let you know."

He pushed the swinging doors and walked in. A bunch of cowboys were drinking at the bar, some playing poker at the tables. He saw no Dancers.

The barman, Bridey, came up to him. He was red-faced and paunchy and wore an apron.

"Whiskey," Slocum said.

Bridey poured a whiskey and stood there mopping the bar.

"I'm looking for Burt Dancer. Seen him?"

The drinkers nearby turned to look at Slocum.

"He *was* here, but he's gone," Bridey said.

A burly cowboy in a red-checked shirt said, "He's gone, but he sure left a mess."

Slocum's green eyes looked at him. "What mess?"

"A bloody mess. Shot up Claws McGrew. Claws came looking for Burt, too. It wasn't much of a fight."

The burly cowboy grinned. "Drink up. It's a short life."

Some cowboys nearby laughed softly.

Bridey was watching Slocum. "See that blond filly? Lorrie by name. She might know something about Burt."

Slocum nodded and drifted over to the girl.

She smiled at him. "What about it, cowboy—interested in a good time?"

"You look like you'd be a lotta fun, Lorrie, but I'm pressed for time. Did you see Burt Dancer?"

"Yeah, I saw him." She grimaced. "He sorta flashed by me."

"Well, I'm looking for him. Did he happen to tell you where he was headed?"

Lorrie ran her tongue over her lips. "You're a good-looking man, mister. Why don't we go upstairs and get real close?"

He stared at her big breasts. "Must say it'd be a pleasure any time but now. I'm in a hurry to catch up with the Dancers."

"Funny thing." Her dark eyes glittered. "Burt was in a hurry, too. No, he didn't say where he was headed. Just tole me to keep him happy."

"A lucky man," Slocum said. He reached into his vest picket for a havana. Then he heard a voice behind him.

"Don't move, mister, or I'll blow your head off."

Slocum froze.

"Raise your hands."

Slocum was startled. The Dancers sneaking up after all? Slocum slowly raised his hands, sneaking a look behind him. Not Burt, but three strangers, men he had not seen before, all holding guns on him. They were looking at him, hard-eyed.

Slocum's teeth gritted. "What the hell's all this?"

"It's about the stagecoach," said the dude in front. He wore fancy clothes and held a bright pistol. He cautiously reached over and lifted Slocum's gun. "There, we stripped the snake of his fangs."

"What do you mean, stagecoach! That's what I'm searching for—the men who held it up."

The fancy-dressed dude had blue eyes which glittered frostily.

"Well, Sheriff Wright thinks you know plenty about that stagecoach. He wanted you in jail till he can get the facts straight. So whyn't you be a good fella and move out quiet-like. We already got your lady in the lockup. Don't make trouble."

Slocum cursed. They had Ellie Mae in the lockup; that complicated the picture. "I'm telling you, cowboy, I had nothing to do with that stagecoach. We rode onto it after it had been wrecked. That sheriff's got a peanut brain."

The dude grinned. "Wouldn't do to abuse the sheriff. He's gonna keep you in jail till we can find out what you did with the bank money. Sent for Judge Murphy, in case we hafta stretch your neck. No funny stuff. Tole me to shoot to kill if you made a break. That you're a dangerous desperado. Fact is, we'd shoot you full of holes right away if we had the gold. So, mosey out of this saloon to the street, and move easy."

He was marched outside the saloon where Sheriff Wright was waiting. He gave Slocum a tight-lipped smile. "You musta thought me an idiot to believe your story, mister."

Slocum's green eyes drilled into the square-jawed face in front of him. "Well, Sheriff, I think you're an idiot, one way or the other."

The sheriff's jaw clenched. "You're talking mighty careless for a man who's gonna swing, soon as you and your female accomplice tell us where you stashed the gold. I know you hid it somewhere out there near the stagecoach. And you're gonna tell us about it before long, I promise you."

Slocum's gaze was calm. "I thought you were an idiot when we first met, Sheriff. But I realize you're not even that smart."

The sheriff brought his fist back to swing, but controlled himself. "All right, men, let's put this smart dude in jail. He won't be talking so funny with a rope 'round his neck."

The cowboys were baffled by Slocum's attitude. He didn't act like an outlaw or talk like one. But they figured the sheriff must know what he was doing. They pushed Slocum toward the jail, a one-story house.

A cowboy with a rifle across his knee sat watching Ellie Mae behind bars. She was fuming. When she saw Slocum, a string of unmaidenly curses passed her lips.

"That sheriff is a dangerous fool," she said.

Slocum walked close to the bars and spoke softly.

"He may be a fool, but he can put a rope 'round my neck and you in jail for twenty years."

She gritted her teeth. "They gonna put you in here, too? Where'd that sheriff get the idea that we did the stagecoach robbery?"

"'Cause he found us there. A simple mind. He found us there, so we musta done it."

"Then he doesn't believe us about the Dancers?"

"If he does, he may think they're on our side."

She swore. "A great sheriff. He's got a slow draw and a slow brain."

"But he can deputize men to hang us," Slocum said glumly. He turned and looked at the jailer, who kept his rifle pointed.

The door opened and Sheriff Wright came in, blue-eyed, bulky, and straight. He might not be much of a sheriff, Slocum thought, but he looked the part.

He stared at the jailer. "Whyn't you put him inside, Billy?"

Billy shrugged. "Didn't know what you wanted to do with him, Sheriff. Nobody told me." He kept his rifle pointed at Slocum. "But he won't do anything or he'd get his head blown off."

Grim-faced, the sheriff fixed his eyes on Slocum.

"Sent for Judge Murphy. He'll give you a quick trial and a quick hanging. But you might as well tell me where you hid the gold. You shot three men. One way or another you're gonna get your neck stretched, Slocum, but you can do a good deed for the lady. She won't have to spend most of her life in prison if you tell about the money."

Slocum gazed at him. "Tell me, Sheriff. You think I did the killing at the stagecoach?"

He nodded. "The robbin' and the killin', Slocum. You and your friends."

"What friends?"

"The friends who shot at me. Jest at me." He shook his head. "That was mighty stupid. Up to that time, I didn't think much of your fancy story about the Dancers, but that shootin' convinced me you were lying. Trying to kill me. If they shot at you, your scheme might have worked."

"Wait a minute, Sheriff. You think I was trying to get you killed? Then why didn't I kill you when I had the drop on you?"

"I thought about that. You weren't going to shoot me in cold blood in front of your female accomplice." He grinned. "She's a gun girl, but maybe she can't stand the sight of blood." He lifted his belt. "Enough jabberin' for now. I got business to take care of. You gonna tell where you hid the money?"

Slocum looked at him grimly. "The Dancers did it, I told you."

The sheriff shrugged. "Your funeral." Turning to the jailer, the sheriff smiled. "That's right, Billy. Keep your rifle ready and don't hesitate to use it. This is Slocum. He belongs in there with his gun lady."

Billy pulled a key from his belt, opened the cage. "Step inside, mister. The lady's lonely, been waitin' for you."

Slocum looked at Ellie Mae and shook his head. He spoke in a low voice. "Put a silver star on a fool and everything goes wrong."

With a satisfied smile, the sheriff gazed at them in the cell. "That's where you two belong. Look natural in there." He turned to the jailer. "Billy, I don't want you goin' close to that cell. Keep five feet away. You hear me now. That man in there is slick as they come. I've met his kind before. No matter what he wants, you're not to get close to that cell. Now I'm goin' to talk to the bank man, Mr. Tobias. Be back later."

He stared hard at Slocum, then grinned. "Thought me a fool sheriff, didn't you? I'm too slick for you, mister." He closed the door behind him.

"I knew that sheriff spelled dumb trouble the moment we met him," Slocum said to Ellie Mae.

"That's not getting us out." She spoke softly. "We got to figure something or you'll be swingin' from a tree and they'll have me in prison for life."

"Why don't you faint?" he said in a low tone. "I'll see if I can grab this cowboy."

She gasped and grabbed at her chest. "I feel faint, Billy. Need water. Quick."

Billy glanced at her. He poured water from a pitcher

into a cup. Then, from five feet away, he flung the water over her face.

She sputtered and raged. "You damned fool!"

Billy just grinned. "Orders—not to go closer'n five feet. She made a fast recovery, didn't she, mister?"

Slocum cursed under his breath. The situation might get serious. What could stop the sheriff, if he wanted, from throwing a rope around his neck? If a sheriff said you were an outlaw, they'd hang you, even with little evidence, just to be on the safe side.

He studied the window. It was high, barred and looked strong. Nothing there. He had a knife hidden in his boot, but he couldn't use it if Billy didn't come near the cell. That sheriff might be stupid, but he knew how to keep a man in jail.

Nothing to do right now but wait. But the longer they stayed in that jail, the worse it would be. Slocum sighed. A rotten situation. Where, he wondered, had the Dancers gone? Probably picked up the loot and were making a run toward Mexico.

He pulled a havana from his pocket and lit it.

Then he noticed the door open just a crack, and Luke Dancer stuck his head in. "Hiya Billy."

Billy swung around with his rifle. "What the hell are you doin' here?" he demanded.

Luke stretched casually. "Come to get these lowdown coyotes off your hands, pardner."

Billy's eyes widened and he raised his rifle, finger on the trigger. "Get your ass outa here before I blow it off, mister."

Luke put his finger to his lips. "Shh, not so loud, Billy." He pointed to the window.

"Tryin' a trick?" Billy said, keeping his rifle on

Luke, but his glance slid to the window. There, big as life, was a head and a hand with a gun pointing at him. "Hi, Billy," said the man.

"Hi, Joad," said Luke.

"Now," said Luke, "if anybody's ass gets blowed off, Billy, I'm afeared it's gonna be yours. And it jest ain't worth you losing it over these varmints. We'll take good care of them. Don't matter who strings them up—you or us." He came close to Billy. "It's a sentimental thing, Billy, that we do it. Matter of personal honor."

Billy's skin prickled while he considered the reasoning. Then, deciding that his own skin was more valuable to him than that of the prisoners, he lowered his rifle.

"That's a good fella," said Luke, taking first the rifle, then the keys hanging on Billy's belt.

Luke turned to the cage, pulled his gun, and held it on Slocum. His eyes glinted viciously. "One wrong move and I'll put a bullet in your gut. A bad way to die. So come along. You both come out nice and quiet. Burt's covering the front and Joad's got your horses at the back of the jail. No funny business." He smiled at Ellie Mae. "Can't let a lovely lady like you rot in jail."

They came out and started for the door. Luke, smiling at Billy, suddenly belted his head with his gun handle. Billy crumpled. "Hated to do this, cowboy," Luke apologized, keeping his gun on Slocum as he lugged Billy into the cell and locked it. "Only way to stop you from yellin' blue murder after."

12

They went out into the night, staying in the deep shadow of the jail building. The street at this time was quiet except for two cowboys talking far down on the porch in front of Bridey's Saloon. For the first time, Slocum saw Burt Dancer close up. He was not big, but sinewy. His round, alert face had steely gray eyes; his body had a slight tilt to the left. He was, Ellie Mae had said, a left-handed gun and greased-lightning fast. His lips twisted in a vicious smile at the sight of Slocum in front of Ellie Mae.

His gray eyes, gleaming in the light of a nearby lamp, stayed hard on Slocum. Finally he said, "You didn't imagine I'd let the law give you a nice little hanging, did you, Slocum?" He shook his head. "Can't let anything *nice* happen to you." He threw a grim look at Ellie Mae. "And here's the little filly who wants to kill us all. Well, we're gonna take good care of you, too, tiger girl."

Far down the street, the two cowboys at Bridey's Saloon mounted their horses and rode west to the other side of town.

"Follow Luke and don't try anything." Burt's voice vibrated with threat.

Slocum glanced at Ellie Mae. Just the sight of Burt had left her white-faced with rage. Fearing she might do something foolish, he spoke softly to her. "Do what the man says, Ellie Mae."

The sound of his voice snapped her rising fury and brought back her good sense. She didn't have a weapon, and Burt, she knew, would mow her down in a moment if she did the wrong thing. With tightened lips, she follow Luke on the dark side of the jailhouse, to the back where Joad had the horses. They swung over the saddles and started riding east, which would get them out of town quickly. Ellie Mae followed Luke; then came Slocum, followed by Burt and Joad.

Slocum felt a curious surge of freedom. He felt the powerful roan under him and the sky above. Yet, in a way, he figured, he'd gone from the frying pan into the fire, into the bloody hands of the Dancers, whose intentions would hardly be friendly. The sheriff would hang a man for a crime, and that would be a pain in the neck for a few seconds. Burt Dancer probably had severe ideas for punishment.

Slocum decided not to worry about it and to enjoy the beauty of the night. A silver moon riding a dark blue sky was throwing its beams all over the craggy mountain ranges.

They rode east, then swung southwest, and after a time pulled up alongside a butte. Joad took care of the horses. Luke made a fire and Burt pulled a whiskey bottle from his saddle pack. He took a long swig, then climbed a high rock nearby to stare back at the trail.

"Expectin' company, Burt?" asked Joad.

"Best to expect trouble," Burt said. "It's gonna come." He sat in the light of the fire, which lit hard lines about his mouth. He studied Slocum and took another long pull at the bottle. "So *you* shot Rafe." He shook his head. "Don't know how in hell you did it. Musta pulled your gun when Rafe wasn't lookin'."

"Got some short rope?" said Luke.

"What for?" asked Burt.

"Gotta tie this polecat's hands."

Burt grimaced. "You worried, Luke?"

"It's smart."

Burt showed his teeth. "If he makes the smallest move, the smallest, I'll put the first bullet in his groin. That won't kill him, just give him pain. He'll scream a lot. I want to hear that. 'Cause this mongrel has done bad things to the Dancers." He looked at Slocum, who calmly reached for a havana in his vest pocket and lit it.

Burt glared at him. "I'm gonna tell you why I got you outa jail. I jest want to understand something. We Dancers never hurt a hair of your head. But you came into our lives, and because of you, the blood of three of my brothers has been spilt." His face distorted as a wave of sorrow went over him. He shook it off. "What black devil made you go against us? That question keeps knocking in my head. We never did a thing to you." The dancing flames made his steely eyes glitter.

Coolly, Slocum puffed his havana. So that was one reason they got pulled out of jail. Burt was the kind of man who killed easily, but who needed answers, too. Slocum blew smoke into the night air. What should he say? Tell the truth? That might get him a quick bullet. Well, there was no easy way he could go, considering the odds. Three men, handy with guns, and he without one. He thought about Rafe and Tim, then looked at Ellie Mae. She sat there sullenly, looking into the fire.

"I'm waitin', Slocum," Burt said.

Slocum shrugged. "Don't have to tell you, mister, but I will. When I rode into Ledville, I had no beef against you Dancers. But there was a cowboy bullying a young fella, insulting him to force a showdown. It was Rafe Dancer bullying Tim Brady, who was just trying to get home. And Tim Brady, though he knew it would be his death, pulled his gun and died. It was guts. He did a thing of honor and he died. To tell you the truth, I thought it was brave, but stupid. Sometimes a man does something brave and it's just plain stupid."

The Dancers were sitting around the fire, Joad and Luke drinking coffee, Burt holding the whiskey bottle. All three listened hard to Slocum, their eyes glowing in the light of the fire.

"I didn't like it, but still it was none of my business," Slocum said.

Joad gritted his teeth. "It sure wasn't. You didn't know the killin's the Bradys did against our people. What right had you to step in?"

"I didn't step in. Rafe didn't like me. He invited me into a poker game, and when I started to win, he had the gall to cardsharp. Fished up an extra ace." Slocum shrugged. "So I called him on it. He lost the draw."

Burt's jaw was clenched. "Don't believe it. You couldn't beat Rafe in a fair draw. You pulled first. That's why you went out on a run."

Slocum shrugged. "If that's how you want to see it."

Burt's face was splotchy with anger. "That's how I see it."

Joad leaned forward. "And how about Seth? Why'd you turn on him? What in hell did he do to you?"

Slocum tapped the ash off his havana. "He did nothing to me, but he was aiming to rape this young lady. *In front of her own pa.*" Slocum couldn't help a small smile. "No red-blooded cowboy was going to let a sinful thing like that happen without lifting a finger."

Burt's face clouded. "Maybe that was *real* justice. To hurt the man who shot down my father in cold blood. 'Twasn't rape—it was justice."

For the first time, Ellie Mae raised her eyes from the fire. "You're a liar, Burt Dancer. Pa never shot anyone in cold blood. It was Clem who went crazy that night and wanted to do the killin'. Pa just defended himself."

"Defended himself! Cold-blooded killing of a life-long friend. And *we* know the reason, Ellie Mae. 'Cause your slimy father was always after Ma. Always. He never forgave my dad for getting there first. We heard the story a hundred times. Finally, your Pa, jealous and hating, killed my Pa to start this blood feud. That's why we Dancers swore a mighty oath. Either the Bradys or the Dancers would stop walking this earth."

Burt's face was twisted with fury. He stopped to take a long breath, and lifted the whiskey bottle to his lips. He seemed calmer. He turned to Slocum. "I had thought the feud was finished, but now you're in it. You've become a Brady, just like you were born with their tainted blood. And you're goin' to die hard, mister. Because it's *you* who brought on the death of three of the Dancers." He wiped his mouth with his sleeve, then his eyes narrowed. "Tomorrow, Slocum, we're gonna tie you to a rock near here, let the coyotes and the buzzards tear you to pieces." He paused and added grimly, "That should give you a good night's sleep."

There was a long silence. Then Joad got up to put more wood on the fire, passing in front of Slocum. Just then a bullet fired from the darkness hit the whiskey bottle in Burt's hand and splintered it.

Slocum's moves were lightning fast; he grabbed the gun from Joad's holster, holding Joad, tightly gripped, in front of him. Another crack of a gun came from the dark and suddenly Joad slumped. Burt and Luke had thrown themselves tight against the butte. Ellie Mae went flat. Slocum, still holding Joad's body in front of him to protect himself from gunfire, let it go, and sprinted out of the firelight into the darkness to the horses. He threw a shot at Burt and Luke, forcing them back to the butte, then slipped over the saddle of his roan, hitting its flanks. Bending low, he galloped west into the dark.

The gun and horse gave Slocum a surge of power. As he rode, he thought of Ellie Mae. He would get back to her at the right time. He couldn't thank the sheriff and his deputies enough for coming after the Dancers, or was it after the escaped prisoners? Slocum was in the dark, behind the butte, beyond their fire.

He rode on, running his hand with pleasure over the muscled flank of the roan. Then he thought of the Dancers. Joad was dead; that put them down to two. But they had Ellie Mae, and they could pay themselves off with her. And that stupid sheriff . . . what did he think now? Did he believe the Dancers were in on the stagecoach robbery or that they came to the jail just to spring their accomplices? That was what a man as dumb and suspicious as that sheriff would believe.

Slocum took a deep breath of the scented night air. He had to keep a sharp eye out for the Dancers and for the sheriff.

And he had to think of how to get Ellie Mae out of the vicious clutch of the Dancers.

Pressed tight against the butte for protection, Burt Dancer looked at Joad lying face down on the earth, blood staining the back of his shirt. Grief twisted Burt's face; now Joad was gone. There was no end of misery for the Dancers. Burt's hand tightened on the gun. If it was the last thing he ever did, he would make Slocum pay.

He looked toward the bulky rocks, where the sheriff was holed up with his deputies. Burt chewed his lip; he had figured the sheriff would come after them in the morning, but not this night. The sheriff seemed driven by something—maybe greed, the reward money. Viciously Burt swore he would do something with that sheriff, too.

He looked at Ellie Mae lying flat, then at Luke also tight against the butte. Luke, too, was looking sorrowfully at Joad.

"We have to shift our ground," Burt said. "This fire gives 'em a target. Ellie Mae, you crawl over here. If I were you, I'd not stand. That sheriff wants to shoot anything that moves. Crawl to us. I'll lay down some fire to keep them from shootin' straight."

Ellie Mae considered her situation. She would be better off in the sheriff's hands than in Burt's. He intended nothing but malice and hurt for her. But it was true the sheriff's men would shoot any moving target. The sheriff figured they were all involved in the stagecoach robbery.

Slocum came to her mind, lifting her spirits. She'd been amazed at his quickness, the way he grabbed Joad, protecting himself with Joad's gun and body. And now, not ten feet away, Joad lay dead. Another Dancer. The score was beginning to even. Yet, looking at Joad lying there, Ellie Mae couldn't help remembering him as one of her playmates in the old days, when the Bradys and the Dancers were real neighbors. Then she thought of her own brothers and father, all dead and gone. What pity did the Dancers show? They killed without remorse. Her whole family had been wiped out. She was almost alone, except for her cousin, John Brady, in Paso. And where was he in this time of trouble? He had to know by this time what the feud had done.

These thoughts flashed through her mind even as she lay there, aware that Burt was waiting.

"Ellie Mae!" His voice was harsh.

She crawled slowly toward the butte, keeping away from the firelight. There was no gunfire. When finally she reached the security of the butte, she came to her feet.

Burt glared at her. "Don't let me ask you *twice* again. We know you want us dead. And it'd be smart to put a bullet in you right now, so me and Luke won't have to worry about a bullet in the back." He scowled. "That's how you'd do it. We know how you used to play games, Ellie Mae. Lemme tell you, I'm keeping you alive because I know that polecat Slocum will come looking for you. You're nothin' but bait. After we get him, bank on it, you're finished."

He glanced at Luke as if to see how he took it. "Maybe Luke's dumb enough to still be sweet on you. But he's a Dancer, first and last. So don't count on any help from him."

He studied the land, then looked at the sky. A heavy bank of clouds was sailing toward the moon. He pointed up. "Those clouds will put us in the dark shortly. Luke, you take her and go for the horses. I'll get Joad and follow." His mouth tightened. "We gotta give him a proper burial."

Luke looked down at the sprawled body and gritted his teeth. "Joad." He ran his hand through his hair. "It was Slocum who did it."

Burt nodded. "Held him as a target. That's why Joad's dead. If it's the last thing we do, Luke, we get Slocum, and give him a mean sendoff."

They stood silent, looking up. Then the clouds swept over the moon and the earth turned dark. Burt reached down, grabbed Joad, and slung him over his shoulder. Luke and Ellie Mae went fast toward the horses. It was impossible to shoot accurately in the dark, and nobody tried.

Burt dropped Joad over his horse, gave the reins to Luke, then swung over the saddle of his own horse.

"Let's ride," Burt said, and they galloped west, on Slocum's trail.

* * *

Slocum woke to the sound of an animal jumping through the brush. His hand snaked to his gun and, at the sight of the white flash, he fired. The jackrabbit squirmed and fell. Rubbing sleep out of his eyes, he cut some brush, made a fire, skinned the rabbit, and pan-fried the meat. He needed to be strong today. He put his coffee pot on to boil. Then he chewed the meat carefully to get all the nourishment. The coffee warmed his gut. It was dawn, and the sun sitting on the horizon sent streaks of crimson fire into the sky.

Slocum thought about Burt. What would he do? Feel vicious about revenge, that's what. He'd just lost Joad, another brother.

Slocum's lips twisted. Burt would be in a jumping rage to catch and destroy the man who always seemed to be there when a Dancer got shot. It would be smart to keep a lookout, but Burt still had to fight the sheriff off. Would he stop for that or go after the man who had just put Joad among the dead Dancers? Slocum was inclined to think Burt would come after him.

His eyes raked the land as he ate. He stiffened. There was movement on a cut in the sun-dappled, shallow canyon. A lone horseman coming his way, was looking down at the trail.

Slocum slipped behind a thick rock to watch the horseman. He kept looking down. Who was he trailing? Who was he? A sheriff's man, scouting? If so, it would be a good idea to pick him up, Slocum figured, and find out what happened after his getaway from Burt. Maybe the sheriff and his men had wiped out the Dancers and grabbed Ellie Mae. Slocum stroked his chin. This rider had already picked up his tracks. It would be best to brace him and find out what he knew. Slocum's piercing green eyes followed the man.

He was well built, wore a beat-up Stetson, a yellow vest, and Levi's. There was dust over him and his horse. Either this cowboy didn't believe in staying clean or he'd been riding long. He seemed wary, as if he expected an attack. It made Slocum more curious. His jaw hardened. This cowboy was looking either for Burt, for the sheriff, or for himself.

Despite his wariness, the rider never did spot Slocum. He kept coming and, at the right time, Slocum stepped out, gun pointing.

"Hold it right there, mister."

The rider was jolted and he frowned. He reined his horse and stared in puzzlement at Slocum. He was square-faced, with light blue eyes and a blond mustache —a curiously familiar look.

"What's the idea?" he demanded.

"Who are you?" Slocum demanded.

The rider bristled. "What's it to you? I'd like to know who you are."

Slocum almost smiled. There was nothing timid about this polecat. "Since I'm holding the gun, cowboy, I got a better right to ask the questions. Who are you tracking? You were doing that."

The rider's blue eyes looked keenly at Slocum, as if he were trying to make a judgment. Then he loosened up.

"You might have the gun, but you don't look like a man who'd shoot a man in cold blood."

Slocum liked the cowboy and hoped he wouldn't be on the wrong side. "Step off the horse so we can talk. I don't want to get a crick in my neck."

The man swung off the horse and didn't try any tricks.

"Are you working with the sheriff?"

Slocum stared directly into the cowboy's light blue eyes. There was slight puzzlement in them.

"No." He grinned. "Are you a wanted man?"

"I'm asking the questions." Slocum paused. "Are you in the Dancer bunch?"

This time there was impact; his eyes glittered and his body tensed.

Slocum spoke calmly. "Throw your gun before you get into trouble."

The rider thought about it. "How do I know you won't shoot afterward?"

"That's the chance you take, mister." Slocum's voice was hard.

The rider smiled. "I'll take that chance." He pulled his gun and with a sudden move brought it up to fire. Slocum's bullet hit the gun, knocking it down. The cowboy jerked his hand as if it had been scalded. He looked at Slocum with eyes screwed tight and, strangely enough, he smiled.

"That was stupid." Slocum kicked the man's gun away. "You coulda been one dead cowboy. Now I'm going to ask you again: Who the hell are you? And why were you following my tracks?"

The cowboy chewed his lip. The last thing he seemed to want to do was to reveal who he was.

Finally he said, "I'm lookin' for Ellie Mae Brady."

Slocum almost smiled. That was why the man looked familiar; he had the Brady look. "That's interesting. And why the hell are you?"

The cowboy flinched, then stared straight at Slocum.

"Don't know who you are, but I don't believe you're in the Dancer bunch. So I'm gonna tell you, and let the devil do his worst. I'm John Brady, kin to Ellie Mae. Got word that she'd lost her dad, my uncle. Came to see what I could do for her. Been trackin' her since Ledville. In Abilene I learned the Dancers had busted her out of jail. I lost the trail up a piece, but picked up your tracks." Brady stopped. "You been traveling with Ellie Mae. You must be John Slocum. I figgered you'd know something."

Slocum nodded. So this was John Brady. He'd come from Paso to help his cousin. A red-blooded cowboy. Slocum could see the family look in his face.

"You figured right," Slocum said. "But why'd you do a damned fool thing, drawing your gun, if you thought that?"

"Couldn't be sure. Wouldn't take a chance. Meant to shoot your gun. But when you shot mine, I knew you couldn't be in the Dancer bunch. They kill first and inquire later." He pulled a plug of tobacco out of his vest and bit off a piece. "So where's Ellie Mae?"

"The Dancers got her," Slocum said.

Brady's eyes glittered strangely. "They got her?" He took a minute to think about it. "That's bad. Very bad, Slocum." His voice had gone cold, as if he thought Slocum had run out on her, and that leaving her with the Dancers was the worst thing a man could do. "How'd that happen?"

Slocum sat on a nearby rock and pulled out a havana. "I'll tell you, Brady. Burt Dancer has a particular hate for me. Since I been riding with the Bradys, the Dancers have been hurt. Dumb sheriff thought me and Ellie Mae did the stagecoach job and locked us up. Burt didn't care to see me get off that easy. He and his brothers sprung Ellie Mae and me from jail yesterday. Burt aims to feed me alive to the coyotes. Nice fella. So, when the sheriff came after us, I made a break." He smiled. "I aim to go back and get Ellie Mae."

Brady rubbed his chin, digesting all this. His face stayed solemn. "You sure must have given the Dancers a lot of grief for Burt to feel like that about you. How bad hurt are they?"

Slocum puffed his havana. "They've lost Rafe, Seth, Diggers, and last night they lost Joad."

John Brady was astounded. "Damn!" He hit his fist into his palm. "You gotta be a hot pistol. I was figgerin' on fightin' a bunch of Dancers, but only Burt and Luke are left." He stopped. "Of course, Burt is the fastest gun in these parts. Streaked lightning." Brady worked his chaw thoughtfully. "It's bad that they have Ellie Mae. They're liable to do something they'll regret to the day they die."

"What do you mean?"

Brady looked far away, at the glowing mountain ranges. "I just hope they don't try anything with Ellie Mae. That's all."

Slocum shrugged. "I'm thinking it might damn well happen. One of them, Seth, already tried. It's what brought me into this feud."

Brady's jaw tightened. He turned away. "We got to get to them as fast as we can."

Slocum stared. "We'll get there."

Brady squirmed. He squinted at Slocum. "We must catch up with those Dancers, fast as hell."

"I'm for getting to her fast, too. But we go about it smart," Slocum said.

John Brady brushed his mustache nervously. "Gotta get there, Slocum, quick as we can."

Slocum shook his head. Something was eating Brady alive. A secret. But he wasn't talking. It didn't matter. Slocum had been ready to go after the Dancers anyway.

His jaw hardened and he flipped his havana. "All right, then, Brady. Let's ride."

13

In the morning, Burt stopped on a piece of rising land facing the majestic sprawl of mountains.

"A good place. We'll bury Joad here," he said to Luke. They pulled their shovels, dug a grave, and lowered the body. After filling it with earth, they stood in silence. Then Burt said, "You were a good brother, Joadie, and we'll make 'em pay blood for this."

Twenty feet away, Ellie Mae watched the climbing sun spill over the crags and peaks of the mountain. She, too, had stood at gravesites and mourned her own losses in blood.

Burt, hard-faced, turned to Luke. "We'd better take care of the sheriff. He'll keep after us. Greedy about

reward money. And I don't want to be thinkin' of him
when I want to think about Slocum." He paused. "Slocum killed Joad, but the bullet came from the sheriff."

Luke nodded and glanced at Ellie Mae. Burt looked
at her too, at her lovely oval face, her deep blue eyes,
her golden hair glowing in the sun. "Such a pretty
thing," he said. "Who'd think she had the sting of a
rattler? She'll bring Slocum to us. We'll keep her till
then."

Burt walked close to her and spoke in a harsh voice.
"Don't even think of crossing us. I'd as soon put a bullet in you as in Slocum. Only when we're through with
you Bradys will the Dancers be able to breathe easy in
the world. Now get on your horse. Remember, any
wrong move, you're finished."

She shrugged and walked to her horse.

As they rode back on the trail Ellie Mae was surprised at Burt's trailsmanship. He moved with care,
rarely in open space, always scouting convoluted land
that could be used for ambush. His crafty moves were
finally rewarded when they spotted four men riding in
the long valley. It was the sheriff and three deputies,
working the Dancer trail and riding a fast pace.

Grim-faced, Burt studied the land. His sharp eye
picked a fine site for rifle fire. He put Ellie Mae back
with the horses, roped her feet and hands so she
couldn't make a run. Then he signaled Luke, pointing to
rocky camouflage. They set themselves and waited,
peering out from time to time at the riders. The sheriff
was riding third position. As he rode, his eyes scanned
the rocky sides of the defile. He said something and the
men pulled their horses. Burt cursed under his breath.
The sheriff had realized the danger of moving into range

of an ambush site, but sent two riders ahead anyway, instructing them to hug the sides of the defile. They rode forward while the sheriff and his deputy waited, rifles ready.

It was a canny move, and it made Burt hesitate, but only for a moment. He could still cut the enemy down to two. He pointed to Luke's target, the nearest man. They waited behind the rocks for the two riders to move into range. Then Burt lifted his head to see the target. The sheriff spotted him and shouted. Luke and Burt fired at the same time. Their bullets blasted the two riders, who were flung violently from their horses. They lay motionless. The sheriff and his deputy fired, too, but it was useless; they were out of range. Burt waited to see if they would try to recover the bodies. The sheriff didn't think much of exposing himself to such deadly rifle fire. He shouted to the other rider and they turned and rode back.

Burt cursed. He had hoped to wipe them all out so he could concentrate on Slocum. Now he still had the sheriff to think about. He stared down the valley. Should he go after the sheriff and get rid of him, or wait for him? He hated to play a waiting game—for the sheriff to come for the gold, for Slocum to come for Ellie Mae. The Dancers practice was to attack the enemy.

Burt pulled out a cigarillo and lit it. He had cut down the guns against him. Would the sheriff go back to Abilene for more men? And somewhere out there, Slocum was skulking, the most dangerous of them all. Best to be ready for him.

"Think we oughta go after them, Burt?" said Luke. "Don't want that sheriff picking up more deputies."

"Don't think he'd do that. Fearful he'd lose us.

Thinks we got the gold. Wants to trap us before we get to Mexico. No, he's not gonna leave for Abilene."

Luke nodded. "Reckon that's what he's thinkin'."

Burt puffed his cigarillo and looked at the deputies sprawled in death. "We've got good position. We got Ellie Mae, and that's gonna bring Slocum. We got the gold, and that's gonna bring the sheriff." He puffed on his cigarillo. "Don't need to look for anyone. They'll come to us."

Luke frowned. "But we don't have the gold, Burt."

"We'll pick it up at the hideaway." Burt's face was grim. "After we take care of a coupla things. Then we'll go for the border and the easy life. Now let's get the horses—and Ellie Mae."

She was sitting quietly, her face a hard study.

Luke felt a bit embarrassed as he untied her. "Sorry about this, Ellie Mae, but Burt won't trust you further than he can kick a mule."

"Don't apologize to her," Burt said sharply.

"I s'pose you killed the sheriff," she said.

"Not yet," Burt said coldly.

He looked at the surrounding land: parched brush, boulders, valleys, and gullies. He would keep Ellie Mae up front and try to lure Slocum out.

They started riding northest. Whenever they reached high ground, and a rock behind which to hide, Burt would snake back and his piercing gray eyes would search the land behind him for a tracker. He had left a clear trail, convinced Slocum would pick it up. But, hard as he searched, Burt couldn't spot anyone.

He made a new decision and circled back toward the defile. As the day wore down, he became uneasy. When they stopped for coffee, Burt scowled at Ellie Mae.

"Where the hell is Slocum? I figgered he'd come busting his ass to rescue you. Reckon you ain't as fascinating to him as I figgered."

"Either that or he's too smart for you," she said, tight-lipped.

"It'd be best for you if he came along," Burt said. "Because if you ain't bait, you're nuthin'. Nuthin' but the risk of a bullet in the back to us."

She smiled grimly. If it came to that, she would not hesitate for a moment. That gun of his had spilled too much Brady blood.

Burt glared. "Of course, you could be useful in the way any woman could. I admit you're a nice hunk of flesh. It'd be dumb to waste you." A grin twisted his face and he glanced at Luke. "I know you want her, Luke. We can both have her. Use her plenty before we get rid of her." He stopped and his eyes searched the surrounding land. "But business before pleasure." His voice was harsh.

Ellie Mae almost shivered. The last thing in the world she would let happen was to yield her body to the Dancers.

Sheriff Wright sipped his coffee and looked at the buzzards flying in a circle about half a mile back. He cursed softly; he knew what the buzzards were about—Smith and Barrett, who had been ambushed by that Dancer bunch. He ground his teeth with rage, cursing himself for letting them ride into ambush. Then he cursed Billy back in Abilene for being such a dumb jailer and letting the Dancers bust out Slocum and his girl. Now he was out here with just Pete as a deputy to face these vicious killers.

Two more big-bellied buzzards swung east to join the grisly fest, and the sheriff bit his knuckled fist in fury. This stagecoach affair was turning out to be a real misery. The sheriff's experience in Creek City had been with small-time lawbreakers, horse thieves, and such. Some killers, yes, but men who killed in drunken quarrels. The stagecoach had been a big robbery, with three men shot in cold blood. The sheriff drank more coffee, wishing he had some whiskey. These Dancers were real desperados and killed without conscience. He had not met gunmen like them. When he snared Slocum and the girl in the beginning, he thought he had a good lead. He hated the remarks Slocum made, but he was convinced Slocum was part of the gang. When the Dancers had busted Slocum out of jail, it supported his belief—Slocum was in the bunch. Until last night. He could see what happened after he ordered his men, if they had a target, to shoot at the Dancers.

One of the Dancers had stood, a good target against the fire. Smith fired at him and missed. Then he saw Slocum grab the standing man, pull the man's gun, and hold him in front of his body for protection. The sheriff fired at that Dancer and didn't miss this time. Slocum went running for the horses, and the sheriff could hear the sound of hooves.

Why would Slocum make such an escape unless the Dancers had vicious intentions? It could turn out that Slocum had been telling the truth, that he had been hunting the Dancers, and they were the mangy dogs who held up the stagecoach. The sheriff realized now he had been wrong on Slocum.

Well, that was water under the bridge. He had to decide whether to go back to Abilene for more deputies.

But the Dancers were only two, after all. The woman would be a drag on them. She belonged with Slocum. The sheriff decided not to go back to Abilene. The Dancers would get too far ahead, impossible to catch. They had the gold with them, and it would be a feather in his hat if he nabbed these stinking hyenas. Just a matter of hunting them down.

He looked at his deputy, Pete Loring. "It was bad judgment riding into that ambush. I figured those robbers, since they had the gold, would make a hard run toward the border. You'd think they wouldn't stop to worry what was behind them. Didn't expect them to ambush."

Pete shrugged. "You never know what the right judgment is till afterward. If they'd been smart, they would have headed for the border, like you said." He looked glumly into the fire. "Too bad about Lem and Jack. Only consolation is they never knew what hit 'em." He lit a cigarillo. "It was bad we didn't stay to bury them. Now those buzzard bastards are gonna get 'em."

The sheriff's square jaw clenched. "Pete, those Dancers were waitin' with rifles for us to pick up the bodies. They're vicious killers. Look at how they shot the men on that stagecoach. Never gave them a chance to surrender and live. You can't make bargains with vicious dogs like that."

The sheriff sipped his coffee again and thought of his wife, Miriam. He had told her this would be a quick job. He could make five hundred dollars in reward money if he got the gunmen who did the stagecoach killing. More, even, if he got the gold back. He figured it wouldn't be that hard. She had gazed at him proudly.

"Rennie, you go out and catch those desperados. We can do a lot of things around the house with the money."

Now he was stuck here, having to figure his next move. Suddenly he thought of Slocum. Damn it, if he had believed Slocum's story, he might have had the help of his gun. Slocum looked like a good man to have on your side.

Then he thought of the Dancers again and the merciless way they killed. "Yeah, Pete, they never gave those stagecoach riders a chance. If a man's a killer, he never gives a man a chance," he said.

"You're dead wrong about that, Sheriff," said a cold voice. "Don't reach for your gun."

The sheriff and Pete whipped their heads around. Two men and a woman came out of the brush behind them. Though the men didn't hold guns, they held their hands down near their holsters.

"You're Dancer, are you?" the sheriff said, standing, as did Pete, to face the men.

The man smiled. He was a round-faced man with strange gray eyes. "That's right. Burt Dancer. This is my cousin, Luke. Never mind the lady. She goes where we go."

The sheriff's strong jaw clamped. This was an amazing piece of luck. The damned idiot had come in without pulling his gun. He had just signed his own death warrant. He shifted his glance to Pete, who understood what they would do, if they had to.

"Well, Burt Dancer, I admire your nerve, coming in like this. You aim to give yourself up. That's the right thing to do. I'll get you a fair trial. Bring in the money, throw yourself on the mercy of the judge. That's the best I can offer."

Burt glanced at Luke, who smiled back.

"You mean a fair hangin', don't you, Sheriff?"

The sheriff shrugged. "Well, you shot three men. Two more yesterday. Deputies. But you can't tell about Judge Murphy. He may think you were gone loco. A man goes loco sometimes and shoots folks. He may give you time in the pen instead of a rope. But you did the right thing, comin' in here like this. So why don't you just fork over your guns and the money, and let's go peaceably back to Abilene."

"You're sorta dreamin', Sheriff," Burt said, smiling, though his eyes were chips of ice. "You shot my brother Joad last night. I'm here to pay you back."

The sheriff scowled, not understanding. If they had come for revenge, why didn't they come in shooting?

"Don't get it, Dancer. You here for a showdown, is that it?"

Burt nodded slowly. "Happen to hear you complainin' that a killer never gave a man a chance." The smile slipped off his face. "I'm givin' you a chance, Sheriff."

He stood absolutely still and waited. The sheriff, amazed, felt the blood surge to his face. Dancer, instead of sneaking in, firing in ambush, hitting him in the back, was ready to meet him head-on. He felt a wave of excitement. The sheriff drew the fastest gun in Creek City and miles around. And this fat-faced little man was laying down a challenge. Wright stared into the dead gray eyes. There was five hundred dollars' reward for this man's carcass. The sheriff went for his gun, watching Dancer's left hand move. It was a lightning smear. The bullet hit the sheriff before his hand reached his holster. He catapulted back and fell. He never even heard the bullet that killed his deputy, Pete.

Ellie Mae, who had been forced to be there because they didn't want her running off, shut her eyes.

To satisfy her feelings, she thought, Burt Dancer deserved to die a hundred times.

14

What the hell was keeping that mangy dog, Slocum? Burt Dancer wondered as he sat at the fire drinking whiskey. They had seen neither hide nor hair of him anywhere. Did he just run scared to save his own skin? Burt wondered if he had been wrong about Slocum. No. He knew that kind of man, a hard head, a trail wolf who never let go once he sniffed your tracks. Oh yes, Slocum would come, sooner or later. Burt smiled viciously as he looked at Ellie Mae in the firelight, all golden-haired and pretty. The bait—that was why Slocum would come. He couldn't let a decent woman fall into a gunman's bloody hands. Burt's face was a sneer as he lifted the bottle to his lips. Slocum already knew that he nursed deadly hate for those who killed his brothers. Slocum had to know there would be no place for him to hide in the territory. So he would have to come and settle it. The trick was to force Slocum out of hiding and be ready. Get him into a draw. Burt knew he was the fastest gun. That's why he was called "Streak Lightning"—the left-handed gun. Of course, he'd never put Slocum away with a bullet. That was too easy. Disable him, fulfill his promise to feed him to the buzzards. Slocum had robbed him of his blood brothers—Rafe, Diggers, Seth, and Joadie. Their names came to Burt Dancer like the tolling of a funeral bell. Dead, all gone, forever. He would never joke and drink with them again. All the times they had had on the ranch around the fire at night—the Dancers—destroyed by this devil come out of nowhere to help Ellie Mae.

Burt looked at her and felt a sharp impulse to grab her, do her great damage. His body went tight with the jolt of his feelings. But he caught himself. *All in due time*. He had learned that when your feelings stampeded your head, you made bad judgments. There would be time to work his vengeance out on Ellie Mae. He thought of her body. A beautiful girl. His face twisted; he had to admit it, though he hated admitting anything good about the Bradys. The time to take care of her had to be right.

He turned to Luke, sitting alongside him, smoking quietly. "Tomorrow, early, we'll ride to the hideout house and pick up the nuggets. No more sheriff to worry about, just Slocum. He'll come. For all we know, that's what he might be waitin' for—for us to dig up the gold. A sly polecat. But it'll do him no good. He'll get his hands on that gold when he gets his hands on Ellie Mae. And that's never."

Ellie Mae stared at him venomously. "Don't be too sure, Burt. Slocum hasn't gone down one time, but a lot of Dancers facing him did. Must mean something."

Burt's hand went out like a snake and slapped her face. She didn't cry out, just stared at him, the mark of his fingers red on her cheek.

"That's brave, hitting a woman. But you were always good at that."

Burt smiled maliciously. "Did me good to hit you, Ellie Mae. 'Cause you're not a woman but a she-devil. And that's what you're tryin' to do now, bedevil me, make me lose my head. It won't help. Slocum will come, 'cause he's that kind of man. And my left hand will take bloody pieces outa him."

There was sudden fear in Ellie Mae's heart. It was true. He was the fastest gun in the territory. How could Slocum beat him? Only by trickery—by getting the edge, shooting from ambush. She hoped Slocum wouldn't make the mistake of pitting himself against Burt because it was sporting. Her heart felt leaden as she recalled his words—"not the sporting thing to do." It would be crazy to come up "sporting" against Burt's left hand! She looked at the butte and the land around, hoping Slocum's rifle would destroy this vicious killer. But nothing moved; nothing happened.

As they packed their gear and put it in the saddle-bags, Burt kept his hand near his holster, studying the nearby crags, the boulders and brush. When he had struck Ellie Mae in sudden rage, he felt at the time it might break Slocum out of hiding. His red blood would surely boil to see that happen to a decent woman. But there was nothing.

Burt grunted, and they started northeast, riding at a fast pace in single file, Ellie Mae in the middle. After fifteen minutes of riding they disappeared around a hill.

Only then did Slocum and John Brady come out of their hiding place, a high rocky perch, too far to shoot, but not too far to see.

Brady had been staring after the Dancers with his fierce blue eyes, and when they disappeared, he cursed under his breath. "Why'd you stop me shootin' that rotten dog, Slocum? Mighta hit him."

"Never could," Slocum said calmly. "Way outa range."

"Worth a shot to find out. How could you stand to see him hit Ellie Mae."

"Didn't like it, but he didn't grab her or do real hurt. Your shot would be wasted and would tell him where we are. That'd be dumb. Now he's edging back toward Abilene. Might be going for the gold."

Brady scowled. "How do you know?"

"If he had the gold, he'd go for the border." He turned to Brady. "It's best to trail him, hit at the right time. Remember, he's got Ellie Mae. He can put a gun on her and force us to do anything. We gotta make a surprise hit."

"If they don't surprise us first," Brady mumbled.

They started back to where the horses had been picketed near a patch of dry brush. "Besides," Slocum said, "I keep hearing Burt's the fastest gun around here. So let's not go in stumble blind."

Brady frowned. "I thought *you* were a hot pistol, Slocum. All those dead Dancers."

Slocum turned. "I just managed to be there when they were killed. I did get Rafe, and set Joad up for a bullet. That's all. Ed Brady shot Seth. And Ellie Mae did Diggers in dirty—a rifle bullet in the back. Not sporting. So you see, I'm not the hot pistol you been thinking."

He walked on while Brady thought about it. When they got to their horses, he said, "But you beat Rafe. And Rafe, they used to say, was as fast as Burt. I remember the games when we were yearlings. Used to be a tossup between them who had the fastest draw."

Slocum thought of how Burt was jolted when he'd heard Rafe had been shot. What did he say? "You musta shot him when he wasn't lookin'."

Slocum smiled grimly as he swung over the roan and started it jogging. In his experience, you didn't know how fast a man was until you pulled against him. It could be too late then. The showdown was a deadly gamble.

So far, by using his head, Slocum had managed to keep breathing in a territory where sudden death by gunfire was the way of life. He didn't think of himself as a great gunfighter. Mostly, Slocum tried to judge his opponent by the signal he sent just before he went for his gun. Most gunfighters unconsciously tipped before they drew, a tightening of the lips, a quiver of the eyes, a twitch of the hand, a tiny betrayal of the mind's command to go for the kill. It was this secret that gave Slocum an edge, because then he had his gun coming up. Slocum did not delude himself: there were gunfighters who were fast, who didn't tip off—the real legends of the territory. Survival in gunfighting was a matter of taking a lot of care.

These thoughts drifted through Slocum's mind as his eyes followed Burt Dancer's tracks.

They followed the Dancer trail northeast, riding until sundown in the shadow of the craggy mountain. They stopped once to refresh the horses, got another hour riding before they pitched camp. They made a fire in a pit, ate venison, and watched the sky darken against the huge, looming mountain. Slocum looked at a hawk circling frantically, its eye on the target below.

Brady acted strangely tense. He said, "I hate every minute Ellie Mae is in the hands of those Dancers."

Slocum looked at the dark sky, lit suddenly with silver stars in the millions. He thought of the mystery of the heavens and wondered if man on the earth made any sense.

"Tell me, Brady, why are you so feared about Ellie Mae?"

Brady glared. "Doesn't it rile you that these kind of men have grabbed a lovely young woman?"

"It does," Slocum said. "Doesn't mean they'll do anything. They've known her since she was a tender shoot."

"They're lowdown dogs, and they want to pay her back for what's happened to their kin."

"Maybe not." Slocum remembered something Ed Brady had said when Seth grabbed Ellie Mae. "It'd be the worst sin in the book." The statement was dramatic and stuck in his memory.

"Brady," Slocum said, "is there a dark secret about Ellie Mae and the Dancers?"

John Brady scowled. "Dark secret? What the hell are you talkin' about, Slocum? Don't want that girl raped by the Dancers—that's what I don't want."

Slocum's jaw hardened. "Burt Dancer strikes me as a man with a business head. First revenge, then the gold. Last and least, the lady. So we'll track 'em, watch 'em, wait for them to get the money. And when the time's right, not before, we'll move in." Slocum's green eyes were cold. "If you don't see it like that, Brady, you're not going to be much help."

Brady pulled out his bedroll. "For the time being, Slocum, I'll try to see it like that. For the time being."

Next morning, Slocum drank his coffee and thoughtfully watched the sun climb, spreading warmth. It looked to him like any other June day. A hawk swooped to earth for its prey, a roadrunner ferociously sprinted to a hole to try to grab a rattler that had stuck its head out, a scrawny coyote scrambled fiercely in the brush after a frantic jackrabbit. Nature, Slocum thought, was fiercely alive and challenging its creatures, those with strength and cunning, to survive another day.

Slocum thought about this as he drank his coffee. He, too, was one of nature's creatures, caught in the survival war, hunting not food but a creature like himself, who also had in mind death and destruction.

He stretched and gazed at the bronzed peaks of the mountain. They would survive this day. John Brady still sat at the fire, drinking coffee. He looked like an older version of Tim Brady, whose death had indirectly plunged Slocum into the Brady–Dancer feud. Since then, a lot of men had gone under. He sighed and looked at his gun—cleaned, oiled, and ready.

The Dancer tracks were going south of Abilene. Slocum thought about it. Burt must be going back for the gold he had salted away. He was too smart a dog to carry it. Anything could happen and he would lose his treasure. The way Slocum figured it, Burt was pushed by two obsessions—to destroy the man who had destroyed the Dancers, and to get his gold.

Burt's movements revealed how his mind worked. Slocum smiled, thinking that he was supposed to rush out pell-mell when Burt struck Ellie Mae. That idea didn't work. Burt had shot the sheriff, who was partly responsible for the death of Joad. Now Burt had to be headed for the gold.

Did it mean he had given up hunting Slocum? Not at all—just that he was working on another scheme.

"So you figger Burt is goin' for the gold?" John Brady said, watching Slocum stretching.

Slocum shrugged. "Burt's got a lot of ideas, and I ain't a mind reader. I don't think he knows about you yet. But what do you s'pose he was doing yesterday, making that big circle, parading Ellie Mae? He was trying to bait me out. And he was ready to bushwhack me." Slocum grinned. "I try not to be stupid, Brady."

He took off his Stetson and the gentle air ruffled his hair. "To survive in the territory, you never move into the web a spider is spinning. Smarter to make the spider come out of his web. Then you got him."

John Brady's face was solemn. "You look like you been through a lot of wars and survived, Slocum. Must know somethin'."

"My bet he's going to the money." Slocum grinned. "It'd be nice not only to nail Dancer but to pick up the stagecoach gold. Don't you think so, Brady? The bank would show its gratitude."

Brady shrugged. "I'm thinking of just one thing,

Slocum, and that's getting Ellie Mae out of the dirty clutches of Burt Dancer."

Slocum's jaw hardened. He was getting tired of this mystery about Burt Dancer and Ellie Mae.

"Then let's try to do that, Brady." He moved toward the roan.

15

Burt Dancer rode northeast at a fast clip. From now on, straight to the hideout house and the money. Slocum would follow. Oh, yes, he'd follow. It was smarter, Burt thought, to bring a mangy dog you wanted to kill into your trap.

As Burt rode, he gritted his teeth. His obsession to shoot Slocum to pieces was now a sickness. He could almost hear his brothers' cry for revenge come out of the earth.

"Won't be long," he muttered through clenched teeth.

As he rode, his sixth sense told him that Slocum was riding behind him—always out of sight, because Slocum was a crafty devil, but Burt knew he was back there.

Now he, Luke, and Ellie Mae rode abreast. And when they hit a high elevation giving a good backward view, Burt didn't bother to look back. It would be a waste. Slocum wouldn't be visible. He was too crafty a trailsman. He had already proved that. A crafty dog, Burt figured, but he'd show his fangs. And Burt knew where. That was where he'd set his trap.

The sun was coming down when they reached the hideaway house, a shack built of logs, set in a clearing of cottonwoods. It was not easy to find.

Luke put the horses out to graze as Burt and Ellie Mae went into the house. Ellie Mae had been hoping all during the ride that Slocum would make an appearance. Now she felt a wave of uneasiness. Only the worst could possibly happen in this house.

Burt had told her plainly what he had in mind. He had no fears. He told her she was bait for Slocum. She would be used as women were used. Then he meant to throw her away, and he would. She knew Burt was loyal to his own kind, but viciously unforgiving to those who injured them. He would kill her, she knew. "There can be no peace for the Dancers as long as a Brady lives." Burt never said anything he didn't mean.

Why hadn't Slocum come? The question nagged her. Did he fear Burt Dancer, the vicious revenge Burt planned, a living death? It was horrible to think about.

Slocum was a man in every sense of the word. He had stirred feelings in her she had never known before. It had been a pity that, because she had been so caught up in the deaths of her brother and father, she couldn't respond to those feelings. She had hoped somehow he would still appear, pull her from this pit of death. She had made up her mind she would die before she let Burt Dancer put a finger on her. The man who killed her people! She'd die. One way or another. Force him to shoot her, resist to the end. Her mind was made up.

They lay flat on the earth and looked down at the hideout house set in a hilly stand of cottonwoods. Slocum looked at the land behind the house, studded with half-buried rocks, thick brush, and short trees. Tricky land, he thought. Three horses grazed in a nearby field. He looked again at the house. It had a window on its left side.

"That's where they are, Brady," Slocum said.

Brady nodded, his mouth tight. "So how do we get in there and cut Ellie Mae loose?"

"Reckon it can only be done over two dead bodies."

"Blasted shame it is," Brady said.

Slocum glanced at him.

"All this needless killin'," Brady went on.

Slocum shrugged. "I thought revenge was the only idea in the Bradys' heads. You should hear Ellie Mae. She's bloodthirsty about the Dancers."

Brady shrugged. "Terrible mistake, all this stupid killing."

Slocum rubbed his chin. He had to remember that John Brady had not lost brothers and a father to Dancer guns, like Ellie Mae.

"Maybe you ought to trot up there, knock on the door, and invite Burt to give up Ellie Mae."

Brady looked embarrassed. "I s'pose guns is the only way."

"You remember the Dancers when you were all playful kids," Slocum said. He thought of the dead men at the stagecoach, dead deputies, dead sheriff. "These Dancers are killers."

Brady looked sad. "It all turned out bad."

Slocum's green eyes studied the house, thinking about how to break in. "We'll do best coming at them front and back. They're not sleeping in there. They're waiting with guns ready. They don't know you're in this, Brady. That's our ace. Ride a wide circle, come from behind the house. Leave your horse on the other side of that hill, move down easy, check everything near you. I'll wait till you reach that boulder to the left of the house.

"By the time you get there the light should be dim. If not, we'll wait. When I raise my hand we both move, quiet as hell. I'll give 'em a chance to see me. They don't know about you. Keep low always. Try to get to the window and pour some lead at the Dancers right off. Don't give Burt a chance, 'cause he'll blow you apart. I'll kick in the door. Burt's in there thinking how to nail me. He's planning a surprise party for me—could be anything; he's smart. One thing, he's got Ellie Mae there, and she's on his mind."

Slocum put out his hand. "Just remember, Brady, Ellie Mae's in with the devil himself, and he wants only the worst for her."

Brady looked a bit unnerved, as though he wanted to say something. He just bit his lips and started out.

He made a wide circle and reached the top of the hill as the sun started to dip. It was splotchy land with thick brush, rocks, and trees. He could see the house below, and the boulder he was supposed to reach. He pulled his gun and crept forward. They had an edge because the

Dancers could not know that he had come to help Ellie Mae.

He looked beyond the house to where he had left Slocum. No sight of him. He looked at the house and its window. The sky was darkening. He crawled ten feet and stopped. His face was near the earth, and he smelled the ground. He could hear the murmur of insects, feel drops of sweat on his neck. Thirty feet to the boulder. Thick brush lay to his left. He crawled forward. He'd be there soon. He paused to look for Slocum's position.

"Hold it there." A cold voice.

Brady froze, then slowly turned. Luke Dancer was holding his gun. He had been lurking behind the thick brush. How long had he been there?

"Luke," he said.

Luke's jaw was hard. "John Brady. You damned fool. Why couldn't you stay put in Paso, where you belonged? Why'd you have to get into this?"

Brady's heart pounded. "Ellie Mae's my cousin, Luke. She's lost everyone. You can't let a girl like that go it alone."

Luke's jaw was hard. "Maybe she's better off without you. Ever think of that, John?"

Brady stared at him. "Were you laying for me?"

Luke shook his head. "No. We were laying for Slocum. Didn't know about you. Where is he?"

"Dunno. He made his own way."

Luke's blue eyes looked skeptical. "Somewhere nearby, of course. Drop your gun."

Brady hesitated, then dropped it. "I've got something to tell Burt, Luke. It's important."

"I'm sorry you got in this fight, John. I've no beef

against you. You been outside the feud, but you just put yourself in." He paused. "I can't let you go. Burt would kill me. We'll go back to the house, see what Burt wants to do." He motioned with his gun. "Move down careful and keep mighty low."

A gunshot cracked the silence and Luke fell. He had been hit in the chest. Brady looked at him, feeling grief, yet aware that Burt wouldn't waste a moment, but would shoot him on sight. Luke had only delayed his execution.

He looked at Luke, whose square face was white and distorted with pain. He was dying.

Brady bent to see if anything could be done. Luke's blue eyes stared at him, glittering with approaching death. Then the gun in his hand barked and the bullet struck Brady. He was flung back, fell, and rolled down.

Luke, in a rage, because he was dying and still young, with nobody else to kill, pulled the trigger of his gun again and again.

Then he died.

Slocum, whose gun had picked off Luke, chewed his lip. His bullet, he realized, had not killed Luke instantly; it had given him enough time to shoot Brady. A rotten deal. He wondered if Brady was finished. He would have to find out. That clever bastard Burt had put Luke behind the house, just in case, and he had lucked into Brady. Slocum ground his teeth. Burt would be inside the house, waiting. It was dark, with a dim sliver of a moon coming up. It didn't take long to reach John Brady.

Brady wasn't dead yet—wounded badly, but still conscious.

"Hold out, Brady. I'll get whiskey and cloths for you."

"Slocum. Gotta tell you something."

Slocum paused. "Let it wait. I'll fix you, then go after Burt."

"No, it can't wait. Bend down. I can't talk well, and I've got a lot to say."

Slocum frowned and put his ear to Brady's lips. He listened. And as he listened, he frowned.

Slocum lay on his belly behind a rock and peered at the house. Burt and Ellie Mae were in there. Burt would soon discover that Luke was gone, and his wish for revenge would be overwhelming. He, too, was alone now, like Ellie Mae, stripped of his family. The fury he wanted to blast at Slocum for all this would be spent on Ellie Mae for bringing in Slocum.

Now there was urgency.

"Luke!"

Slocum could hear Burt's voice, pitched hoarse because of his fear. He had heard shots, and his visibility from the house couldn't be good. He didn't yet know.

Slocum considered what to do. If he revealed Luke's death, it would unleash Burt's rage. It would hit up against Ellie Mae.

After a few moments, he heard Burt's voice again, with pain in it.

"Slocum! I know you're out there. Answer me or I'll kill Ellie Mae. You've got one minute."

Slocum's fist tightened on his gun. "Don't do that, Dancer."

Pause. "What happened out there?"

"Luke shot John Brady." He hesitated. "Luke's dead, too."

There was an awful silence. Then came the crash of a bottle against a wall and a strangled cry of pain.

Slocum studied the house—just a window, if he could get to it, but Burt would be moving from door to window, to make sure he would pick up Slocum before he reached the house.

He lay quietly, trying to think what Burt would think.

"Slocum!"

"Yeah."

"I've got a sporting proposition." Burt waited, then said, "I got two sacks of gold in here, and Ellie Mae. She's naked as a jay. Gold and a beautiful woman. Why don't you come and get them?"

Slocum's face was grim. Burt had a vicious sense of humor.

"Sounds good, Burt, but what about your gun?"

"Here's the proposition. You come in here. We'll talk. I got something to say. Then we'll draw. Winner takes all, the girl and the gold. That's the sportin' proposition. Fair enough? Otherwise, I'll kill her and come out after you anyway."

"It's sportin'. But how do I know you mean it?"

Pause. "I mean it. Ellie Mae will call out if I'm holdin' a gun. She's not afraid—won't lie."

Slocum considered it. Sure, Burt could beat everyone in a draw. He wouldn't have to be tricky. And he was that kind of man, willing to gamble fortune and life on his quick draw. Slocum had met killers who would put their lives on the line just to prove that.

"All right, Dancer. Kick open the door and stand where I can see you."

Burt laughed. "How the hell do I know you won't have your gun out?"

"If I'm gonna take your word this sporting proposition is on the level, you'll have to take mine."

There was silence.

Then the door was kicked open.

From his grounded position behind a rock, Slocum looked in. No Burt. Not yet. Then a piece of him showed and stopped. Slocum's face was hard as he, too, moved into view, his hand near his holster.

As if satisfied that Slocum meant to keep their contract, Burt walked casually into center view, ten feet back from the door, strong hands at his sides, but away from his holster. His eyes were like a hawk's.

Slocum came forward slowly.

Burt didn't move, just watched.

Slocum stopped at the doorway. Burt still stood at ease, but motionless. On the table were two bags of gold nuggets. Back against the wall was Ellie Mae, her hands tied. She was naked. It was a jolt, and Slocum's eyes quivered.

It almost made Burt smile.

"I didn't pull my gun then, Slocum, though the timing would have been right. You can relax." His face twisted again in what was meant to be a smile, though he was so chewed up inside he couldn't smile right. "You see, I don't have to use any tricks. You can't beat me in a draw. But I admire your guts for coming in here. 'Cause you're practically dead. But there's no hurry." He glanced at Ellie Mae. "Look at that woman. Feast to the eyes, isn't she?"

Slocum felt Burt wanted a fair showdown—a matter of vanity, that's how he was. He looked at Ellie Mae. She stood there without fear or shame. Her skin gleamed in the lamplight.

Burt ran his tongue over his lips. "Peach of a woman, isn't she? Sort of a shame you ain't goin' to touch her. But you can dream on it while you're hangin' like buzzard food on a tree. I promised you that, and Burt Dancer keeps his word. While you're hangin' there, jest keep thinkin' how ole Burt Dancer is enjoyin' Ellie Mae—a bitch Brady who, like all the other Bradys, is gonna go outa this world, after she pleasures me."

Slocum's green eyes drilled hard into Burt. "Know why I mostly came in here, Dancer? To tell you that just before John Brady died he gave me a message for you. Something you oughta know before you touch Ellie Mae."

Burt looked at him skeptically.

Slocum's voice was soft. "He told me that Ellie Mae is your half sister."

There was a terrible silence. Slocum didn't take his eyes off Dancer.

Burt's body shook with the violence of his feelings. "I oughta shoot you to pieces now for that rotten lie. But I'll do it soon enough."

"A dying man's words are never a lie," Slocum said, speaking evenly.

He stepped back, putting space between himself and Burt. "I'm goin' to tell it to you the way John told it to me. Word for word. He said your mother, Martha Jane

Davis, and Ed Brady were in love long before your father, Clem Dancer, came along. Brady had gone on a cattle run to Kansas City, meant to come back and marry your mother, Martha. He came back too late. Ellie had been born, put secretly with John Brady's mother. Martha married Clem Dancer, thinking Ed Brady was gone or dead. To console Brady, she gave him the child, who she intended to adopt. Brady raised Ellie Mae and kept the secret. Trouble is, your father found out one night, while playing cards with Ed Brady, and pulled his gun. But Brady was faster. That started the feud."

Burt Dancer had been listening with growing horror. It had to be true. He'd always been jealous of the way his mother treated Ellie Mae, of her softness to Ed Brady. All the boys resented her feelings about Ed Brady. So that explained it. It had to be true. He ground his teeth.

What did it mean? To hell with it! The one clear thing was that Ellie Mae had brought Slocum in and he mowed down the brothers. He had to pay.

Burt faced Slocum. "It don't matter. She doesn't count in this game. It's you and me, Slocum. Since you came in the Dancers have gone down. It's your turn now. And you ain't goin' easy. Pieces of you."

They backed slowly away from each other, hands at their sides. Slocum's concentration became white-hot. He was up against Burt Dancer and he needed every edge.

And Slocum searched for it, the tipoff a gunfighter sent just before his hand started to his holster. And he saw it, the sudden hardened jaw in Dancer's face. The signal! Slocum's gun was on its way up, but the left hand of Dancer moved, a lightning smear. Both shots sounded almost as one. Burt, convinced he had the greater speed, shot for Slocum's shoulder, to immobilize him, then to shoot the rest of him at leisure. His bullet hit true, but Slocum's bullet hit its target, too— the heart. Burt vaulted back and fell against the wall, looking up at Slocum, who was holding his shoulder. A look of amazement came to Burt's face. When he died, the expression was still stuck there, steel-gray eyes shocked by the idea that he'd been beat in a showdown.

Slocum turned to Ellie Mae.

"Oh God, Slocum," she said, and ran to him, her nude body pressed hard against his.

Their mouths and bodies came together. He responded to her velvet flesh, her silky buttocks, and felt a great swelling in his groin.

"Hold it," he said. He pulled Burt out of the door, threw a blanket over his body, then rushed back in.

"I wanted you," she murmured as he threw off his clothes.

His shoulder was bleeding slightly; he tied a kerchief around it, and turned his attention to her.

Her body coiled about his like a snake, and his hands were all over her, her lips all over him. They rolled and twisted and squirmed. He pierced her moist warmth, and ecstatic sounds escaped from her. He stayed with her while she screamed softly into his flesh, her body jumping wildly. Finally Slocum hit the stars.

They lay quietly for a while.

"Let's do it again," she said.

They did.